"I DON'T LIKE THE LOOKS OF THIS," PARKER SAID.

JAKE LOGAN

SLOCUM AND THE BIG THREE

JOVE BOOKS, NEW YORK

SLOCUM AND THE BIG THREE

A Jove Book / published by arrangement with
the author

PRINTING HISTORY
Jove edition / April 1999

The Penguin Putnam Inc. World Wide Web site address is
http://www.penguinputnam.com

ISBN: 0-515-12484-2

A JOVE BOOK®
Jove Books are published by The Berkley Publishing Group,
a member of Penguin Putnam Inc.,
375 Hudson Street, New York, New York 10014.
JOVE and the "J" design
are trademarks belonging to Jove Publications, Inc.

PRINTED IN THE UNITED STATES OF AMERICA

10 9 8 7 6 5 4 3 2 1

1

Austin Pritchard was trying to work up the nerve to blow his brains out, when a man came in through the window.

Pritchard had been expecting that somebody would come for him. That was why he had fled here, to this squalid room in a cheap hotel in the waterfront district of River City, Missouri. But he'd thought his pursuers would come by the door, not the window. The room was on the second floor.

The single room held a bed, a night table, a chest of drawers, a writing table, and a chair. Pritchard sat at the table, facing the door, which was locked and bolted from the inside. On the table top before him was an oil lamp, a bottle of ink, some writing paper, and a gun. Pritchard held a pen in his hand, with the gun within easy reach. A few lines were scrawled across the top of a piece of paper.

The lamp burned a crude grade of oil, giving off a sputtering sooty golden-brown light.

Pritchard was tall and soft, with wavy inky-black hair and a smooth pale face. His hair was now thatched and disordered. His eyes were red-rimmed, feverish. They kept glancing up from the notepaper to the door at the slightest noise, real or imagined, that came from the hall outside.

Behind him and to the side, a window stood open, a square of blackness that was night on the riverfront. There were sounds of distant steamboat whistles and buoy bells. From time to time, a breeze blew off the water, lifting the window curtains and bringing into the close room the smell of the river, humid and dank and underlaced with the scent of something rotten.

Outside, a clock-tower bell tolled the hour, nine o'clock of a midweek night. Reflexively—for he was a punctual man—Pritchard took out his pocket watch to make sure it was keeping correct time. When he lifted the lid, he saw that the watch had stopped some hours before. In the excitement of recent events, he had forgotten to wind it. He couldn't recall the last time he had done that. He was a methodical man.

He reached for the winding stem, abruptly stopping himself. Why bother? He'd run out of time. His remaining life could be measured in minutes—seconds, if he heard them coming up the stairs for him, for that was all the time it would take for him to snatch up the pistol and shoot himself in the head.

He looked at the watch. It was a good one. Solid gold, the way his future had seemed less than three days ago. At least the watch was still good. He'd have liked to leave it to his kin; they could have used the money it would bring.

"Too late for that now," he said to himself. "Whoever finds the body will probably steal the watch. Why not steal from the dead? It's even easier than stealing from the living," he muttered under his breath, laughing bitterly.

He went back to the note. While he'd been thinking, an ink blot had fallen from the stylus point to the paper.

"Damn!" he said, for he was an orderly man. He

reached for the paper, ready to crumple it up and throw it away and begin anew, but—

"No, no," he said aloud, shaking his head. "Might not be time to write another note. This'll have to do. Still, one hates to display poor penmanship, even in a suicide note!"

Something seen in the corner of his eye caught his attention. He looked back, over his shoulder at the window. The curtains were moving. *The wind,* he thought, and then he saw the gun.

It reached in from outside, thrusting through the open window into the room. Pritchard stared at it. It swiveled to cover him, a short-barreled big-bore revolver held by a steady hand.

Its owner followed it into the room, folding himself almost double to step through the square opening, then unfolding himself to his full height once he had both feet on the floor.

He was a big man, strong, fit, hard. He had a wolfish face with green glittering snake eyes and a neat mustache. He looked like Satan. Pritchard glanced at his forehead for horns, but the stranger wore a hat. He wore an expensive tailored suit and custom boots, a shining white shirt, brocaded paisley vest, and a fancy cravat. His neat barbering and elegant attire bespoke something of the dandy in him.

By comparison, there was nothing fancy about the gun. It was all hard lines and blue steel, with a big black hole at the tip of the muzzle. The front sight post had been filed flat for a quicker draw, but that detail was lost on Pritchard.

Pritchard's jaw dropped, his mouth gaping open. The stranger put a finger across his lips, motioning for silence. He came deeper into the room, creeping noiselessly as fog.

Pritchard had been too astonished to react, but now, as the stranger neared, looming up at him from across the table, he remembered his own gun. He grabbed for it, but the stranger was quicker, scooping it up in his free hand.

Pritchard tensed himself for a lunge. The stranger's gun wagged at him admonishingly. "Uh-uh," the stranger said, shaking his head. Pritchard sagged, sullen, not cowed, looking for his chance.

Still covering him, the stranger backed to the door, checking to make sure that it was locked. He paused, listening, hearing nothing that alarmed him. He flashed white teeth in what could have been a smile. To Pritchard, it had all the warmth of a hangman's rope.

The stranger crossed to the table. He perched on a corner of it, resting a hip there, a gun in each hand. The guns were pointed away from Pritchard, but not so far that they couldn't cover him in an eye blink.

"You're Pritchard," the stranger said, not asking, but stating a fact. His voice was low, intimate, with something of the West in it, a note that was not unusual in this riverport town that was a gateway to the frontier.

"Yes, I'm Pritchard," the other said, pleased to note that his voice held firm, steady. Now that the end had come, he would face it like a man.

"Go ahead and shoot. You'll be doing me a favor," he said.

The stranger's eyes and mouth turned up at the corners. "Are you in such a hurry to die?" he asked, sardonically amused.

Pritchard waved a hand dismissively. "I wouldn't want to keep your masters waiting. I know they're eager to cross me off their account and leave a clean slate."

"My masters," the stranger echoed. "And who might that be?" His tone was mocking, as if he were playing a cat-and-mouse game.

"You know. Claggard, Truax, and Detheroe," Pritchard said.

The stranger leaned forward, thrusting his face toward Pritchard. Underlit by the lamp glow, all weird shadows and hollows, it looked more devilish than ever.

"Claggard, Truax, and Detheroe. Fine fellows all," the stranger said, sneering. "What business would such captains of industry have to do with you or me?"

"They sent you to kill me," Pritchard said, unflinching.

The sneer shaded into a smile. "Since when do respectable businessmen need hired killers?" asked the stranger.

"Since when are those three respectable businessmen?"

"If you thought that way, Pritchard, what'd you throw in with them for?"

"I didn't know what they were until it was too late, after they'd swindled the bank out of all its money and left me holding the bag!"

The stranger chuckled. "That's not what the law says. There's a warrant out for your arrest right now, on a charge of embezzlement. You're wanted for stealing the funds out of the Emporium Bank."

"Yes, that was a very clever finishing touch on the part of Misters Claggard, Truax, and Detheroe. Not content with pillaging the bank funds, they arranged things so that I would be blamed for the theft!"

"Why not? You're a trusted officer of the bank, you had access to the vault—"

"So did they!"

"Try telling that to a judge and jury," the stranger said, his sneer returning.

"I don't suppose I'll have to worry about that," Pritchard said, glancing significantly at the other's gun.

The stranger shrugged. Pritchard swallowed, suddenly dry-mouthed. "I thought they might send someone like you. It'd be like them not to leave any loose ends. Me sitting rotting away in a prison cell isn't quite so sure as me dead,'' he said.

The stranger used a gun muzzle to turn the note at an angle, so he could read it. It said:

> To my dear mother and sister—please forgive me, this is the only way out

That was all that was written. The stranger looked questioningly at Pritchard.

''I won't be taken alive by the law, to be dragged through the courts like a common criminal,'' Pritchard said. ''At least I can spare my family that.

''Or rather, you can. It's better this way. Now I won't have the sin of self-murder on my soul,'' he said. ''But I warn you to look to yourself, my friend.''

''Oh? And why's that?'' asked the stranger.

''Your masters may decide to settle accounts with you as they have with me. Leaving a paid assassin alive is just one more loose end, and as we both know, they don't like loose ends.''

''Man, you're green,'' the stranger said, shaking his head. ''You're really some kind of horse's ass, Pritchard. No wonder the Big Three was able to give you such a riding.''

That roused Pritchard from the apathy of despair. Eyes flashing, twin spots of color glowing in his cheeks, he said, ''Here, now, there's no need to add insult to murder!''

''You're almost too dumb to live at that, but I'm not the one to kill you, Pritchard.''

''What are you playing at?''

The stranger eased himself off the table corner, standing up. He pushed back a flap of his jacket, dropping the short-barreled gun into an ingenious holster-sling rigging high on his hip. When the jacket had fallen back into place, the gun made a barely noticeable bulge.

He still held Pritchard's gun, pointing it negligently in the other's general direction.

"If you're toying with me, playing some kind of cruel game, I warn you it won't work," Pritchard said. "I don't care if I live or die."

"Then you're a damned fool," the stranger said. "You've got me wrong, Pritchard. I'm not your executioner."

"No?" the other said, scoffing. "Then who are you?"

"The name's Slocum. That mean anything to you?"

"Slocum," Pritchard repeated, thoughtful, frowning. "That does seem familiar, but . . .

"What of it?"

"I own twenty-five thousand dollars worth of Emporium bonds. Or at least, I did," Slocum said. "Come to think of it, I still do—own them, that is. But the money the notes are drawn on is gone.

"That leaves me with twenty-five thousand dollars worth of worthless pieces of paper. Twenty-five thousand dollars. I guess that's not much, compared to a half million in missing bank funds."

"Actually, it's a little under four hundred thousand," Pritchard automatically noted, for he was a precise-minded man.

"Four hundred thousand, is that right? Still a lot of money," Slocum said. "That twenty-five thousand was a lot to me. It wasn't so easy to come by either.

"Sure went fast, though."

Pritchard stared, incredulous, but seesawing towards belief. "You—you're not from the Big Three?"

Slocum shook his head. "I told you, I'm a bondholder. But I guess you wouldn't remember the name, on account of it's just a matter of an itty-bitty little piss-ant twenty-five thousand in notes.''

"Wait—Slocum, yes, that does sound familiar. . . .''

"Well, hallelujah. If I'd known what kind of mooncalves would be watching my money, I wouldn't have put it within a thousand miles of your damned bank,'' Slocum said.

"Then you—you're not going to kill me?''

"Why bother, when you're so all-fired hankering to do the job yourself? I'd give you a boot in the tail, if I thought it'd kick any sense into you, but from where I stand, it's not worth the trouble.''

"Why'd you come in through the window?''

"Because that's how I like to do things,'' Slocum said harshly. "Playing the other fellow's game got me a skinning. Now I'll play the game I know.''

"What game is that?''

Slocum smiled, the meanest smile yet. Pritchard stifled a shudder. "What do you want with me?'' he asked.

"When the bank failed, I went after some of the officers. The ones bigger than you,'' Slocum said. "I was too late. Baker's gone.''

"Gone? You mean, run away?''

"I mean gone, vanished. Nobody's seen him for days. And another trustee, Calhoun, was found hanged this afternoon.''

"Calhoun, hanged?!'' Fists balled, Pritchard started up from his chair, nearly upsetting it.

Slocum cut him off with a curt gesture of the gun, saying, "Sit.''

Pritchard sat, his face and body twisted with emotion. "Calhoun dead! I know he was the Judas, the one who threw the vaults open to the looters! I'm glad he's dead—

but—but he wouldn't hang himself. He wouldn't have the nerve to take his own life.''

''He's not stupid enough, you mean,'' Slocum said. ''I'm inclined to agree with you. I lifted the sheet when they were carrying him out of his house on a stretcher. His face was all bruised, like he'd been beaten. Of course, he might have beaten himself up before sticking his head in a noose, but I don't figure it that way.''

Pritchard squeezed his face, trying to massage some life into it. It felt numb.

''Calhoun was guilty surely,'' Pritchard said, ''but not Baker. I can't believe it. He wouldn't steal a penny.''

''He's probably sitting on the bottom of the river,'' Slocum said.

''No! He was a good man, a gentle man.''

''Like you said, the Big Three don't like loose ends. You're the only one left. I wasn't sure about you, Pritchard, about where you stood in all this. Now I know you're nothing but a dupe.''

''I'm starting to get the idea myself,'' Pritchard said, smiling weakly. ''How'd you find me? I thought I'd covered my tracks fairly well.''

''It was easy. Anybody who wants to find you badly enough can do it. And I'll tell you something else. I wasn't the only one looking. I got here first, but the others aren't far behind,'' Slocum said.

''Others? What others? You mean the law?''

''Them too. But I meant some of that Big Three crowd. I reckon they'd like you to go the way of Calhoun and Baker,'' Slocum said. He went to the window, crouching beside it.

''What're you going to do?'' Pritchard asked.

''Leave the way I came in,'' Slocum said, placing a foot on the windowsill.

"Wait!" Pritchard jumped up. "What about me?"

"What about you?"

"I'm an innocent man!"

"Too damned innocent."

Pritchard took a step forward, freezing when Slocum said quietly, "That's close enough."

"But you can help me clear my name!"

"Listen up, sonny," Slocum said, snorting. "You know and I know who looted the bank: Claggard, Truax, and Detheroe. But knowing and proving are two different things. You'll never beat them in a court of law. They're too smart for that. If you live long enough to get to court."

"You don't have to gloat about it," Pritchard snapped.

"Not gloating, just thinking that you're sure showing signs of fight for someone who was ready to throw in the towel a few minutes ago. Throw it in? Hell, you were ready to strangle yourself with it.

"Maybe there's hope for you yet," Slocum said. "I doubt it, but who knows?"

He broke open the revolver, swinging out the chamber and letting the bullets fall to the floor. They plopped on the carpet like iron peas from a pod. He tossed the empty gun on the bed.

"Here's your gun. You can kill yourself, or you can fight," Slocum said. "If you fight you'll probably get killed anyway, but it's more fun if you make them work for it."

He ducked through the window, stepping out on to a ledge and disappearing. The opening was a blank black square framed by listlessly rippling curtains.

After a pause, Slocum stuck his head back in.

"Don't waste time looking for the Big Three in River City," he said. "They've left town. Gone west. Used all that bank loot to buy themselves into a Colorado railroad."

"How do you know all that?" Pritchard demanded.

"This isn't the only window I've climbed into tonight," Slocum said. "Mountain Valley, Colorado. Ever heard of it?"

"No," Pritchard said.

"That's where you'll find Claggard, Truax, and Detheroe. Unless I find them first. See you," Slocum said.

Then he was gone.

2

"Good heavens, what a dreadful place! And the people—! I ask you, Clarissa, have you ever seen such desperate characters in all your life?"

"Oh, it's not as bad as all that, Aunt Ethel."

"It's worse! Some of these brutes look as if they'd cut one's throat for the price of a drink, or merely for fun."

"I'm sure they're all very ordinary law-abiding citizens."

"Pshaw! They're a pack of rogues, fools, and knaves. You can see it in their faces, stamped there like the mark of Cain."

"Please, Auntie, you're embarrassing me."

"Look at that one, he looks like the very devil himself!"

"Shhh, he'll hear you!"

"Let him. Speak the truth and shame the devil, I always say!"

Slocum had heard the conversation. His ears were good. He turned his head away, so the ladies wouldn't see him smiling. There were two of them, a young one and an old one. Aunt Ethel was a pigeon-breasted dowager with icy eyes that stared disapprovingly down a long patrician nose.

13

Her niece, Clarissa, was a pretty brunette, sweet-faced, sensible, and nubile.

Slocum, the women, and a handful of others were gathered at Arrow Point, a landing on the east bank of a river in north central Colorado, at the foot of the eastern face of the Rocky Mountains. The site was south of Denver, north of Pueblo, and west of both towns. There were no towns here, just a couple of wooden-framed buildings and shacks on a knoll overlooking the point. None of the structures stood completely upright, all of them slanting in some degree away from the strictly vertical.

The point was shaped like an arrowhead, with the tip angling slightly upstream. The river ambled across the landscape in a lazy S curve. From the landing to the other side was a hundred yards or so. Here, the river was broad and flat, about eight feet deep in the center. It ran smooth as green glass. Further upstream and downstream, the watercourse narrowed, running faster with patches of rapids and rough rocks.

On the west bank of the river, woods came down almost to the water's edge. Beyond lay the mountains, titan walls of gray-black rock rising to blue-white peaks.

The east bank lay at the edge of a grassy plain dotted with thickets of wood. A dirt road ran north-south, paralleling the wide looping course of the river. A second road stretched from the landing eastbound across the plain and over a distant ridge.

The dirt roads crossed beneath the knoll. At the end of the point, a floating dock jutted out into the water. Moored to it was a flat-bottomed barge, the only way across the river short of swimming it.

On each bank stood a wooden scaffold tower housing a system of pulley wheels. A double length of cable-like rope stretched from tower to tower, spanning the river. The rope was joined together so it formed a continuous loop.

In the center of the barge stood a pillarlike framework holding pulley wheels. Both the upper and lower lengths of rope were threaded through the mechanism.

The arrangement of ropes and pulleys was like a giant clothesline, except that instead of hanging wash out to dry, it moved the barge back and forth across the river.

The rope was heavy. On the ground, there were ring-topped posts to support it, but most of its length was strung out in a long, wide, shallow curve that grazed the water.

The barge made two daily scheduled crossings, once in the morning, once in the afternoon. It was now mid-morning, and the barge would soon set off. Not long ago, a stagecoach had stopped at the knoll station, disembarking a half-dozen passengers and their baggage before continuing on its way.

Slocum had come by horse, riding a gray stallion named Steel. Three weeks and hundreds of miles stood between him and that night in River City when he'd confronted fugitive bank cashier Austin Pritchard. He'd left town that night, westbound. That was the last he'd seen of Pritchard. Two weeks later, a week-old newspaper had informed him in a small item, not much more than a paragraph, that the wanted man was still being sought, and that an arrest was "imminent."

Further west, in the vast immensity of the plains, the problems of the Emporium Bank and its swindled shareholders shrank into a dot of nothingness. No echo of the event had reached the inhabitants of the prairie towns and villages that were ever more sparsely strung along the railroad lines that plunged deeper and deeper into the frontier. If it had, they would have said that it served the investors right for trusting their hard-earned cash to an octopuslike entity as slippery and treacherous as a bank. Slocum wasn't so sure but that he wouldn't have agreed with them.

He'd ridden the train west, angling through Kansas to the Colorado border. There he'd gotten off. At a trading post, he'd outfitted himself for the trail. He'd bought the horse there too, for a good price. Mountain Valley was enjoying a boom. Booms raised prices. The nearer he got to his destination, the more things would cost. So he'd bought as much as he could at that little hamlet on the state line. He needed to stretch a dollar. That bank disaster had cut his operating funds down to the bone.

One thing he hadn't needed to buy was weapons. He had plenty of them. He'd bought plenty of ammo, though.

He'd traveled on horseback the rest of the way, camping out at night. It had helped toughen him up, shaking out the slackness and softness that had come from too much high living in the pleasure palaces of the glittering river cities.

Living rough on the trail, sleeping out under the stars, sure was a tonic. Now he was so sore and ornery from riding all day and sleeping in a bedroll on the hard ground at night, that he was starting to feel like his old self. Wary, hard-eyed, on the prod. Putting a bullet into somebody would be a pleasure.

That was just about the right frame of mind for tackling Claggard, Truax, and Detheroe.

First, though, he had to get across the river. That was why he was now waiting for the barge at Arrow Point to begin loading.

Gone were the dude clothes of the one-time River City swell. He now wore a dark high-crowned hat, black leather vest, pine-green shirt, brown jeans, and boots. A lethal Colt was holstered low on his right hip. The gunbelt and the gun weren't new. They'd seen service before, and were in top working order.

He'd used the gun to get rich. Now the money was gone, but he still had the gun.

Hidden under his vest was a souvenir of city life, the blunt short-barreled revolver in its custom sling. He wore it on his left side, butt-out, accessible to either hand. It was a good gun, so his River City sojourn hadn't been a total loss.

A few more such deadly surprises were hidden on his person. He was a great believer in hole cards.

He stood to one side of the landing, holding his horse by its head harness, keeping it clear of as much of the pre-boarding commotion as possible. The animal was a scrappy mountain pony, not overly large, but rangy and surefooted, with lots of endurance. That would come in useful later, on the hairpin trails scaling the heights.

He gentled the animal, rubbing its long head. The horse seemed to like it, nuzzling his palm. Part of its equipage was a saddle gun, a Winchester rifle in a scabbard. Slocum had owned the piece for a long time. Neglect had caused it to go slightly out of true, but he had sighted it in properly before hitting the trail. Now it shot straight. He hoped he could lose his own inner rust as easily.

The landing was crowded with passengers and cargo, ready for boarding, including a supply wagon drawn by a two-horse team. The wagon was manned by two ranchers named Sutton, a father and his grown son. They were locals, known to some of the crossing idlers and hangers-on, with whom they passed the time of day while waiting for the boarding to begin.

The stagecoach had kept its distance from the landing, discharging passengers and baggage at the station, on the level ground atop the riverbank. It was left to the passengers to get their baggage down to the landing. There were always a couple of loafers hanging around the station, willing to tackle baggage-handling chores for a few coins. One way or another, the baggage got moved.

Piled up to one side of the head of the spit were mounds of luggage: carpetbags, handcases, and trunks. Grouped around the mounds were the owners.

Those who had come in on today's coach included Aunt Ethel and her attractive young niece, Clarissa; Tiverton, a tight-lipped, closed-faced businessman; Meachum, a traveling salesman with a pug nose and red face; and a tall, husky, athletic young man with a smooth-shaved, open face.

Also present, waiting to make the crossing, were a couple of burly workingmen and a lone individual who seemed to be a preacher. The workers were en route to the mines, where there were jobs to be had. They were without horses, and if they had ever had any, they had sold them long ago and far back on the trail, for the men showed signs of having made a long overland tramp. They were dirty and unshaven, their clothes tattered. There were two of them, and they called each other Mack and Jack. In grimy stony faces, their eyes were hot and bright.

The apparent preacher was tall, fiftyish, with bushy gray eyebrows and thick sprouting muttonchop side-whiskers the color and texture of steel wool. He wore a black hat with a rounded crown and flat brim, a turned-around collar, and a long black three-quarter-length coat. The coat was oversized and baggy, and hung on him like a horse blanket. A couple of buttons fastened it closed at the middle.

He stood in the shadow of the cable-rope tower, holding a bible open in both hands. He was reading some passages aloud to himself, moving his lips as he mumbled his way through them. He kept to himself, and everybody else ignored him.

The bargeman and his helper came down from the knoll

to the landing. The bargeman, Big Joe, was bearlike, massively thick in the arms, shoulders, and trunk. His helper, Tiny, was a big hulking galoot, taller than Big Joe but thinner, with too-close eyes and a turnip nose.

Big Joe stood aside while Tiny handled the boarding chores. The barge was a rectangular-shaped raft, fifty feet long and fifteen feet wide. It looked like a couple of barn doors joined together, floating on a bed of braced crosstimbers. The top of the raft was planked over. It stood about a foot above the waterline. The sides were bordered with waist-high rail-fence barriers. The walls at the short ends were hinged gates.

There was an order to loading the barge. First came livestock, then cargo, and then passengers. The elder Sutton sat up in the front of the wagon, holding the reins, urging the team forward, toward the barge. Big Joe moved to stop him, Sutton reining in to a halt. The wagon was loaded with supplies, and Big Joe was worried that it'd be too heavy for the deck planking. Sutton argued otherwise. Big Joe was unyielding. Sutton climbed down from the wagon and went to the barge with Big Joe. The younger Sutton stayed behind, holding the horses.

Sutton senior and the bargeman climbed around the deck, examining the planking. They straightened up, standing face-to-face on deck, arguing back and forth.

The sun climbed, hot in a blue sky. In Colorado in September, the days were hot and the nights were damned cold. That was on the flat, which was a mile high, here at the base of the mountains. Higher up, it was colder.

The sky was cloudless, the sun strong, intense.

Sutton paid Big Joe an extra coin on top of the fare. Suddenly there was no more problems, and the rancher was free to bring his wagon on board. He had to do it without the bargeman's help, though, for as soon as the coin was in Big Joe's hand, he went back to sitting in the shade.

Tiny opened the loading gate, and he and the two Suttons got the horses and wagon across the boarding ramp and onto the barge. When the wagon was on board, the team was unhitched and tethered in a forward stall, partitioned off from the rest of the boat like a goat pen. The wagon was placed to one side of the central pillar holding the pulley works. Heavy stones were jammed under the wagon wheels, wedging it in place.

Slocum's horse was the only other animal making the crossing, so it was the next in line to come aboard. Big Joe stood to one side of the open gate, holding his hand out palm-up. It was as big as a roofing shingle. Slocum dropped a coin into it and Big Joe let him pass.

The raft was like a giant floor sticking out into the river. Holding the horse's bridle, Slocum guided it along the barge's right side, the side facing upriver. He went forward to the barge's front end. It couldn't be called the bow because it was bow and stern both, depending on which direction the barge was moving.

The horse was on the front starboard side of the barge, Sutton's team was on the port-side front, and a broad center space stood between them, split down the middle by the double loop of the tow-cable rope stretched across the river.

Slocum tethered the horse to a rail post and stood beside it. Hooves clopped on the planking, sounding hollow. Through spaces between the boards beneath his feet, Slocum could see water sloshing under the raft.

Next came the cargo, crates of stuff to be ferried across the river. Freight wagons carted them to the east-bank station, and on the far bank there was a station serviced by the Mountain Valley carters, but between them lay the water. The bargeman was paid to move cargo across it.

Big Joe and Tiny manhandled the crates onto the barge. They were coffin-sized and -shaped and heavy. Labels and stencilling identified their contents as machine tool parts and similar hardware. It seemed likely that they contained what they said. Nobody would risk shipping anything valuable unescorted.

Grunting and groaning, the bargemen wrestled the crates into place in the starboard center of the craft, balancing them against Sutton's wagon on the port side.

On the landing, fidgeting impatiently, Tiverton hauled out a gold pocket watch and flipped open the lid. It was a heavy watch with a thick gold chain, both glinting yellow in the sunlight. Tiverton looked at the timepiece, snorting irritatedly. "Late! A damned nuisance, that's what I call it!"

A tugging at his sleeve made him look behind, where the preacher stood almost at his shoulder.

"It's later than you think," the preacher said solemnly, blinking pale blue watery eyes.

"Eh? What's that?" Tiverton said, somewhat taken aback.

"There's still time to come home to the Lord," the preacher said.

"Er, yes. Quite," Tiverton said. He looked around, noticing that the two workingmen, Mack and Jack, were hungrily eyeing his glittering gold watch. Harrumphing, he put it away and sidled off at a tangent that took him away from the preacher and the laborers.

The last of the crates was loaded, and now the passengers could come aboard with their baggage, once the ferryman had been paid. Big Joe wore a kind of pouch hanging at the end of a leather strap that hung down from his bull neck. The box-shaped container had a hinged lid. It held the gold and silver coins that the passengers used to pay their fare.

Coins clinked in the bottom of the box as the passengers came on board.

3

Meachum, the sales drummer, stood near the end of the dock, drinking from a half-pint bottle. He gulped thirstily, greedily, draining it. He smacked his lips, rolling the taste around on his tongue.

He raised the bottle to his mouth again, but it was empty of all but a few droplets. When the bottle was upended, they clung to the inside of the glass, not moving. He scowled, cursing.

The preacher crept up beside him, saying, "Wine mocketh, but strong drink is a rager."

"Huh?" Meachum said.

"It's not called Demon Rum for nothing, brother."

"One of those, eh? Well, it's done, so you don't have to worry about it," Meachum said, tossing the empty bottle into the river. It sank, bobbed to the surface, and floated downstream.

Aunt Ethel and Clarissa had four pieces of luggage: two carpetbags, a hard handcase, and a medium-sized trunk. The soft bags belonged to Clarissa, who traveled light. Aunt Ethel was not so minded, and the two heavier pieces were hers.

23

Aunt Ethel said, "Please help us get our luggage aboard, bargeman."

"Pay first," Big Joe said, holding out an open palm. Years of cable-pulling had left his hands as rough and knobby as a washerwoman's knees.

Aunt Ethel paid over the fare for herself and her niece, the bargeman making the coins disappear in the pouch box. Aunt Ethel began, "Now, we can handle the traveling bags ourselves, so if you'll just be so kind as to move the trunk and handcase . . ."

"Can't do it, ma'am. I got a barge to run," Big Joe said.

Aunt Ethel colored, stiffening. *"Well!"*

Seeing her face, Big Joe hastily backed away, saying, "I'll have it brought aboard later, when everything's ship-shape and stowed away. I can't leave the barge now."

"Apparently chivalry is dead west of the Mississippi after all!"

"I don't know nothing about that," Big Joe said, stubbornly shaking his head. "All I know is I've got business to tend to before we can get under way, and there's nothing I can do for you before it's been tended, thank you kindly and very much!"

Before Aunt Ethel could let out another squawk, Tiverton broke in, saying, "More delays! You're already almost an hour late!"

Big Joe grinned. "I ain't late at all, mister, not one leetle bit, since I go when it suits me and not a minute sooner. Now, relax and don't get yourself into an uproar, everybody, because we'll push off when I'm good and ready to go."

"Bah," Tiverton said, but he paid and got on board the barge. Aunt Ethel threw her hands up in disgust, stalking off to where Clarissa waited beside their bags.

"Impossible man!" Aunt Ethel said, loud enough for Big Joe to hear it. He leered pleasantly in her direction.

She shuddered, showing him her stiff straight back. Clarissa laid a hand on her aunt's arm, smiling. "It's not the end of the world, dear," she said. "We'll just have to pay someone to carry them on board."

"I suppose we must," Aunt Ethel said tartly. "If we have to wait for a *gentleman* to assist us, our bags will still be waiting here come Judgment Day!"

Big Joe called, "Just hold on to your horses, ma'am!"

"Hmmph!"

Aunt Ethel and Clarissa were approached by the tall, athletic young man, who'd been standing nearby. He had an honest, open face. He wore a derby hat and sturdy town clothes, but had the bowlegged stance and easy rolling gait that came from much time spent in the saddle.

He took off his hat and held it in both hands. "Beg pardon, ma'am, but I couldn't help overhearing you. I wonder if I might be able to lend you a hand?"

Aunt Ethel's face lit up. "Why, yes, you may, young man! And thank you very much!"

He bobbed his head. "Glad to help out, ma'am." He fitted his derby down tightly on the top of his head. He stooped, squatted, took hold of the trunk handles, and straightened, sweeping up the trunk and slinging it over his right shoulder. It didn't seem as if it had been any strain doing it either. His hat was knocked a little off balance, and he patted it back to the desired angle before hefting the heavy handcase in his other hand.

"My, that is impressive," Aunt Ethel murmured.

"Shucks, ma'am, there's nothing to it," he said. "Shall we go?"

"By all means." Aunt Ethel marched down to the barge in triumph, with Clarissa and the young man in tow.

"So you found somebody to carry it after all," Big Joe said, sneering.

"Yes, no thanks to you," Aunt Ethel said frostily.

"Just so's it got done," he said.

She and Clarissa got on the barge. Big Joe stepped in front of the young man, saying, "You got to pay."

"How about I set these down first?" the young man asked mildly. The trunk slung across his shoulder was carried as lightly as a bedroll, without a tremor. He wasn't even breathing hard. These facts were not unnoticed by Big Joe.

The young man continued smiling pleasantly.

"Okay," Big Joe said, "but then you pay."

"Sure," he said. He went on board the raft and stowed the trunk and handcase in a bin in the middle of the craft. Big Joe and Tiny stood at opposite ends of the raft, watching the young man until he went back to the stern and paid the fare.

There were benches lining the rails amidships on both sides of the raft. Aunt Ethel sat on a bench on the starboard, upriver side. Clarissa stood beside her, a hand on the rail.

The young man rejoined them. "Thank you," Aunt Ethel said, bestowing a stiff little nod of approval.

"Yes, thank you so much. You've been so very helpful," Clarissa said.

"Glad to oblige, miss," the young man said.

Clarissa handled the introductions. "This is my aunt, Ethel Crenshaw of Boston, Massachusetts."

"Glad to know you, ma'am," he said, touching his hat.

"And I'm Clarissa Deane, lately of Boston, but a native Denverite."

"Glad to know you," the young man said, touching his hat again. "Mighty glad." He smiled. He had a nice sunny smile that made his eyes crinkle.

"I'm George Parker. George Leroy Parker," he said.

Standing nearby, forward of the trio and with his back to

them, Slocum stood at the rail looking across the river, his thoughts elsewhere. He was planning, his brain seething, turning over schemes. He was ignoring the conversation, which came to him in snatches, but the name George Leroy Parker fell on his ears with a thud, registering.

George Leroy Parker. His eyes narrowed. Where had he heard that name before? He thought, but came up blank.

He shrugged. Wherever it was, if it was important it would come back to him. If not, to hell with it.

Aunt Ethel was saying, "From the way you talk, I'd guess that you're an Easterner, Mr. Parker."

"That's right, ma'am. Originally I hail from New Jersey."

Clarissa said, "You're a long way from home."

"Don't I know it!"

"Do you miss it?"

"I've been out here for a long time. This is my home now," Parker said.

Aunt Ethel said, "I've never had much use for the place, but even New Jersey is preferable to this!" She threw her hand out, indicating by a gesture that all "this" included the barge, the river, the mountains, and beyond.

"Don't you like the West, ma'am?"

"I'm still reserving judgment, Mr. Parker, but so far the signs are not encouraging."

Clarissa said, "No one told you to pack up and mother-hen me all the way from Boston, Aunt Ethel."

"Heavens, child, I had no choice! What else could I do? You were bound and determined to see your father no matter what, and I couldn't let you go traipsing across the continent by yourself, without a proper chaperone!

"You're a very stubborn and willful young lady, Clarissa, and once you got it into your head to go off on this cross-country trek, there was nothing for it but that I should have to come along as your escort.''

Clarissa said, ''I'm sure Mr. Parker doesn't want to hear about our little squabbles, Aunt Ethel.''

Parker, thoughtful, said, ''Deane . . . You did say your last name was Deane, miss? There's a Colonel Deane, who heads the Red River Railroad. . . .''

''He is my father,'' Clarissa said proudly.

''And my brother-in-law,'' Aunt Ethel said dryly.

Parker nodded. ''The colonel's a mighty famous man in these parts, in the West.''

''He's one of the greatest railroaders ever,'' Clarissa said.

''So I've heard,'' Parker said, smiling. ''And I know a little something about railroads myself.''

''You do!'' Clarissa leaned forward, saying, ''Are you a railroad man, Mr. Parker?''

''Not directly. But I'm a great believer in railroads, miss, a great believer!'' Parker rubbed his fingertips against his temple. ''I'm surprised that the daughter of Colonel Deane travels by coach and barge, though, instead of making the trip in style on the high iron.''

Aunt Ethel nodded. ''I couldn't agree with you more, Mr. Parker. Why we're braving the perils of the wild, when we could be riding in a private Pullman car, is a mystery to me.''

''We came almost all of the way by rail,'' Clarissa explained, ''but the bridge is out downriver, cutting the line.''

''The bridge is out? That's funny. It hasn't rained lately, so there couldn't be any flooding,'' Parker said.

''Yes, that is odd, isn't it?'' Clarissa agreed. ''The men on our side of the line thought it was quite strange too. They sent repair crews to fix it, but the work will take days. I didn't want to wait, so I took the overland route.

"Why, you're frowning, Mr. Parker! Is something wrong?"

Parker was evasive, reluctant to speak. "It's nothing, I'm sure, and I sure don't want to worry you ladies, but—"

"But what, Mr. Parker?" demanded Aunt Ethel in clipped tones. "Come, speak up, let's have no more of this shilly-shallying."

"Well . . . what with the gold mines, and the boom town, and the two railroads and whatnot, this part of the country attracts a pretty rough crowd. There's some bad hombres running around loose."

"Heavens, sir, you alarm me!"

"I don't mean to, ma'am, but you're the one who called for some plain talk," Parker said. "Mountain Valley's got more than its share of outlaws, robbers, and thieves.

"But it's not as bad as all that," he added quickly, trying to lighten the mood. "There's some beautiful country and some mighty nice people."

"I hope we meet them soon," Aunt Ethel said, casting a cold eye around the barge and its occupants.

"We've already met one nice person," Clarissa said. "Mr. Parker."

"Uh, thanks. I think you're mighty nice too, Miss Deane."

"Please, call me Clarissa."

"Come, Clarissa, don't be burdening Mr. Parker with a too-forward overfamiliarity," Aunt Ethel said.

"Oh, no, not that. I wouldn't think of it, dear," Clarissa said, straight-faced.

A squabble arose at the loading ramp. Aunt Ethel turned her head to the side, scowling at the disturbance. "It's that dreadful bargeman again," she said.

Big Joe was arguing with the laborers, Mack and Jack.

"We don't have enough for two fares," said Mack—or was it Jack?

"One of you can ride and the other can swim," Big Joe said.

"We've got almost all of the money. We're just a little bit short."

"Fine. One of you can ride, and the other can hold on to the barge and swim alongside. Now, if you're not going to pay up, step aside and let the preacher man through."

The workers stepped aside, huddling with their heads together, talking in low urgent tones. The preacher came forward.

"You can pay, can't you, Preacher?" Big Joe said.

"'Tis better to give than to receive, my son," the preacher said, in a gravel voice.

"Pay, unless you can walk on water."

The preacher turned out his pockets, finally finding a coin for the ferryman.

"It would be an act of charity to make up the difference for those two," Big Joe said, jerking a thumb at the laborers. "They're only a few coins short of the fare."

The preacher smiled thinly. "The Lord helps those who help themselves."

"Ain't that the way of it? Come aboard, Preacher."

The preacher boarded the barge. "That's the last of them, save for you two," Big Joe said to the two tramps. He stood with his hand on the boarding gate, ready to close it. "You coming or not?"

Mack and Jack looked at each other, reached the same conclusion, and nodded. They hurried to the barge, forking over their fares. Big Joe made a show of counting out all the coins.

"What do you know? You had the full fare after all. What a surprise," the bargeman said sarcastically.

The tramps came aboard. The bargemen made ready to cast off.

4

Big Joe went up and down the length of the barge, making sure that the horses were properly secured, the cargo stowed, the passengers safely along the sides, and the rope-ways clear of all obstructions.

Tiny cast off the mooring lines, which had been looped over the top of the pilings. He hopped back on the barge. The loading gate was closed and locked.

There was a slight current of a few miles per hour, barely enough to affect the barge's big bulk even if the towropes hadn't been keeping it in place.

Big Joe and his helper took up positions on a platform aft of the pillar holding the pulley works. A three-foot-long lever jutted out of the side of the mechanism. Big Joe threw it, releasing a clutch that let the gearwheels spin freely.

The bottom half of the looped towrope was threaded through the pulley wheels, feeding into the pillar fore and aft. The bargemen took up a stance aft of the pillar, with Big Joe forward and Tiny behind him. They took hold of the thick towrope and began heaving away at it.

Pulley wheels turned, taking the slack out of the towrope. It tautened, creaking and groaning. The bargemen hauled away at the line, like teamed partners in a tug-of-war. They worked together, in unison, setting up a steady rhythm.

The pulley wheels needed greasing. They squealed and brayed as the rope worked its way through the guts of the mechanism. The noise made a number of birds start from the trees where they had been perching.

The bargemen supplied the motive force: manpower. The pulleys applied that force, harnessing it into forward motion along the cable towropes.

The barge inched forward, ponderous, elephantine. At first it raised a half-inch bow wave. The bargemen kept hauling, heaving away at the line hand-over-hand. The stern of the craft was now a stone's throw away from the shore. The birds that had been startled by its lurching into motion had found new perches in the tree boughs.

The bow waves were now a few inches high. The barge advanced slowly, like a juggernaut. It was halfway to the center of the river.

The rope was running hot through the pulley wheels. Big Joe dashed a bucket of river water over them, cooling them down.

The towropes sang. Out on the water, there was a slight breeze. It was cool and fresh and smelled of the green woods across the river. Sunlight glinted on the water.

Once the barge had gotten some momentum, Big Joe and Tiny eased off into a slow, steady pull.

Slocum looked across the river. Beyond the far bank lay wooded foothills. The depths of the woods, where shadows fell, were black-green.

There were clearings in the green that edged the west bank, most notably in the place inland from the tow-cable tower. Beyond lay a way station, a lesser version of the one on the knoll. It couldn't be seen from the water.

There was movement on shore, figures. Nothing unusual

there. Crossings and stations draw people, especially in the wilderness.

The raft was at the midpoint of the river. There was a sound like a plucked bowstring, only louder, much louder. It hung quivering in the air above the water.

The line connecting the barge to the towrope tower on the far bank sagged and went slack, sinking into the water.

The line had parted. Suddenly freed from all resistance, the rope whipped through the barge pulleys at high speed, whirring like a giant hornet's nest. Coils of rope spilled from the works, piling on the deck.

Big Joe and Tiny had been hauling away when the rope parted. They were thrown off balance and knocked on their asses, tumbling off the platform into the after area.

It was funny, in a way. Meachum must have thought so. He laughed out loud, but he was drunk. Mack and Jack laughed too. It was a good one on Big Joe, too good to pass up.

The barge plowed ahead a few yards, abruptly coming to a stop due to the great length of rope weighing it down.

The horses were skittish. Not spooked, not yet, but skittish. Their eyes bulged and their nostrils flared as they pawed the deck boards.

The boat drifted to a halt in midstream, anchored by the weighty towrope.

Big Joe and Tiny had been knocked head over heels, tumbling like dice. Big Joe crouched on deck, on hands and knees. Tiny lay sprawling. He moved his limbs, groaning.

With the pulleys stilled, it was very quiet. Water slapped against the side of the barge.

On the far bank, a couple of mounted men rode back and forth. It was too far away to make out who they were.

"I don't like the looks of this," Parker said.

The preacher came up behind Big Joe and kicked him in

the ass, a really hard boot in the tail that sent the bargeman sprawling. Big Joe raised himself up on his arms, turning his head. The preacher came around to his side and brutally kicked him on the point of the chin. Big Joe dropped, motionless. The preacher kicked him in the ear.

It all happened fast, like lightning. The preacher had gone about his work with ruthless efficiency.

He tore open his coat. Under its oversized folds was a sawed-off shotgun, hanging point-down along his side, held in place by a sling. He brought the weapon up, leveling it.

He was in a good position, standing at the stern with no one behind his back. From where he stood, he could cover all the others. That double-barreled shotgun could wreak havoc. It had a powerfully intimidating effect.

He had the drop on them, on Tiny, Mack and Jack, the two Suttons, Parker, Clarissa, Aunt Ethel, Tiverton, Meachum, and Slocum. He tapped the tops of the sawed-off's twin barrels.

"You know what these can do," he said. "Anybody want to try making a play? No?"

Apparently not. Everybody was looking at everybody else to see what they'd do, but nobody was doing anything. That was understandable. Slocum was careful to keep his hands held well away from his sides.

Meachum, sunk deep in thought, suddenly looked up as an idea burst forth within his alcoholic brain.

"Shay, you ain't no preacher," he said.

"No? Well, I'll pray for you anyway," the "preacher" said, sneering.

Tiverton, sputtering, said, "What the devil is the meaning of all this?"

"It's a holdup," Parker said glumly.

"You're not so green as you look," the preacher said.

Tiverton said, "A holdup? You mean a robbery?"

"No," the preacher mocked, sarcastic.

"It's a damned outrage!"

Aunt Ethel vented a sound that was a cross between a groan and a shriek.

Clarissa gripped her aunt's shoulder, white-knuckled. Tiverton was rigid with indignation, his neck muscles standing out like pipes. Parker looked troubled, but he held himself loose, easy.

Between Mack and Jack, Mack was the shorter and dirtier of the two. He started laughing.

The preacher, not amused, said "What's so funny?"

"This is a holdup, right? Well, my partner and me ain't got no money!" Mack said.

"Then I'll just have to kill you," the preacher said. He spoke matter-of-factly, as if passing the time of day. He sounded convincing, though.

Mack stopped laughing, the laughter choking off in his throat. Jack edged away from him, until stopped by a wag of the shotgun in his direction.

"Where you going? You stay put. I like it better when everyone's bunched up together. Saves on shotgun shells."

"Don't kill me, Preacher," Mack pleaded. "I ain't worth wasting a shell on."

"Keep your mouth shut and do as you're told, or you'll get what the bargeman got—and worse! That goes for all of you," the preacher said.

"You're no preacher," Meachum said.

The Suttons stirred restlessly, freezing as the preacher started toward them, the deck creaking beneath his tread. He took the elder Sutton's gun from its holster and tossed it overboard, raising a little spout where it entered the water. Young Sutton's gun got the same treatment.

"Over there with the others," the preacher said, gesturing with the shotgun.

The Suttons sidled off in the indicated direction, joining the others on the starboard side. The preacher was herding them together and forward.

He worked his way over to Slocum, always keeping a clear field of fire with the shotgun, never letting any of the others get behind him.

His pale blue eyes were startling in his bronzed weathered face. Bushy gray brows lifted, his eyes widening, then narrowing as he got a good look at Slocum.

"I know you," he said. "I've seen you around before."

"Could be. I've been around," Slocum said evenly. He caught his breath when the shotgun barrels poked him in the belly.

"Easy," the preacher said, reaching for Slocum's gun, pulling it from the holster.

"Don't toss it in the river, it's a good gun," Slocum said.

The shotgun barrel jabbed Slocum hard in the short ribs. Pain knifed across his face.

"Shut up," the preacher said. Whatever he saw in Slocum's face, he didn't like. He took a step backward, leveling the sawed-off in one hand and Slocum's gun in the other.

Slocum stayed where he was and the preacher recovered, once again confident, heedless.

He said, "You sure got mean eyes, brother. The last time I saw eyes like that, they were on a rattlesnake coiling itself to strike. It was swollen, all puffed up with its own poison. I blew it's damned head off.

"What you got to say to that, friend? Hey! What you got to say about that?"

"You're doing the talking," Slocum said.

"Damn right. Maybe I'll do some talking with this, shoot you with your own gun. That'd be a hell of a note!"

The preacher waved the gun around. He looked at it as if seeing it for the first time. He weighed it in his hand, liking its heft and balance.

"It *is* a good gun," he said, grinning. "I'll keep it." He stuck it into the top of his belt, wedging it down. "Walk soft, friend. I don't like snakes," he added.

Slocum didn't say anything. The preacher had missed Slocum's second gun, the short-barreled revolver worn high on his hip, hidden by the leather vest.

The preacher was in a hurry to get to the prosperous-looking Tiverton. Tiverton said, "You must be mad to think you can hold up this barge all alone!"

"I'm doing it, ain't I? Besides, who said I was alone?"

On the far bank, at the water's edge, a wall of green rushes parted, split by a longboat that suddenly struck off from shore. In it were about a half-dozen well-armed men.

Long oars and canoe paddles churned the water as the boat angled downstream toward the barge.

"Here come the boys now," the preacher said. "Not that I needed 'em. From where I stand, this don't rate no more than a one-man job.

"The only one who'd have shown fight was the barge-man—hell, he'd have to. It's his barge. That's why I took care of him first. As for the rest of you . . ."

He spat.

Tiverton said, "You won't be so boastful when the law catches up to you."

The preacher jabbed the shotgun muzzle into Tiverton's belly, hard. Tiverton folded up, his face lead-colored.

"Maybe I ought to just blow you to hell and gone," the preacher said. "Maybe I will." His fingers dipped into one of Tiverton's inside jacket pockets and lifted his billfold. He opened it, eyes widening at the sight of a fat wad of greenbacks. He pocketed it.

Tiverton stood hunched forward, hugging his middle. His face had lost some of its grayness. He was sucking for breath.

The preacher stole his watch too, tearing open the man's vest pocket with the same violence with which he grabbed for the timepiece. He held it by the chain. In the sunlight the metal looked molten. "Solid gold," the preacher said, kissing it before he put it away.

He looked to see where the boat was. It was halfway to the barge.

The elder Sutton started toward Tiverton, freezing when the preacher swung the shotgun to cover him. "Where do you think you're going?" the preacher asked.

"That man needs help," Sutton said.

"No, he don't. He's doing fine. You stay put, or you're gonna be the one needing help."

Tiverton let go of his middle with one hand to wave Sutton back, gasping, "I-I'm all right. . . ."

"See? He's doing fine," the preacher said, grinning.

The boat was nearer. Mack, eyeing it, said, "You sure got a big gang, Preacher."

"Shut up," Jack said out of the corner of his mouth, standing next to him.

The preacher was in a good humor. "We need all them guns to handle you desperadoes."

"Seems like it'd be pretty slim pickings for you all. Don't hardly seem worth it," Jack said.

"We'll find something worth keeping," the preacher said. His gaze fell on Clarissa, becoming harder, crueler. "Won't have to look too far neither," he added.

"I'll scratch your eyes out," Clarissa said.

"Will you now, missy?"

Aunt Ethel said, "Now see here, you vile creature—"

"Quiet, you old crow. It's the sweet young quail I'm interested in," the preacher said.

Parker, frowning, took a step forward. "That's enough of that."

Now he came under the shotgun. "I was wondering when I was gonna hear from you," the preacher said. "You look dumb enough to try to play hero.

"It just goes to show you, nobody takes you seriously until you kill somebody. Well, I can fix that."

"Me too," Slocum said. He stood nearby, in a kind of a crouch, with his back half-turned to the preacher. His left arm was raised, his right hand gripping the gun hidden on his left side. He had a clear field of fire.

He didn't bother to draw the gun, he just jammed it deeper into the holster and twisted it upwards, holster and all. The hammer was shrouded, so there was no danger of it snagging.

He fired, the gun blasting.

5

The round took the preacher just below the hat brim, in the middle of the forehead. His hat flew off, into the air. So did the top of his skull.

He died instantly, before he could trigger off the shotgun. He hit the deck hard. The sawed-off landed on its side with a hard crack, but didn't go off. It fell out of his hand, landing a yard away, near the side of the raft.

A red haze hung in the air where the preacher had stood: blood mist.

A tremor of fear shook the horses. They started, shuddering.

A gray-white puffball of gunsmoke hovered in midair above the raft.

The outlaw boat was near, only a few lengths away. When the shot had sounded, they'd thought it had been their man pulling the trigger. So it hadn't mattered much.

Then the preacher had gone down. In his flat black hat and long black coat he'd made a distinctive figure. There was no mistaking him for somebody else.

The outlaws paused, oars and paddles in hand. The boat kept on gliding forward, toward the barge.

The preacher's hat landed right side up in the water, and started drifting downsteam, slowly, lazily.

Then time stopped, seeming to be standing still, and things started happening.

Slocum drew his smoking gun and dropped deeper into a crouch, facing the oncoming boat. A man sat on a stern-post, raised up above the others, holding a rifle across his chest. He was bringing it around when Slocum shot him. Slocum fired twice. The first shot smashed into the side of the rifle, caroming off it. The second shot took him in the chest. He fell back, flipping off the boat into the water.

Parker grabbed Aunt Ethel's arm with one big hand and Clarissa's with the other and ducked, pulling them down to the deck with him, trying to get them out of the line of fire.

Somebody shouted "Take cover!" and then everyone on the raft was in motion, scrambling, dodging.

The horses bucked, kicking, trying to break free, iron-shod hooves hammering the deck plates.

Some of the outlaws got their guns into play, popping off shots. Slugs thrummed through empty air, sometimes smashing into some part of the barge's deck works, sending splinters flying.

Slocum had three more shots. He pumped them into the boat, hitting three men. One was a sure kill, and the other two were certainly slowed up for the moment.

He dove headfirst to the planking, keeping his head down, flattening an instant before the outlaws sent a mass of bullets at him. The sides of the barge were raised eighteen inches above the deck, a thick solid-wood bulwark against the rounds that harmlessly bored into them.

He didn't dare to raise his head up, or any other part of him. He broke open the gun, swinging the cylinder out and spilling the spent rounds on the decking. There were spare rounds in his vest pockets. He dug out a handful and started reloading.

The outlaw boat was right on top of the barge.

Parker bellied across the planks, to the sawed-off shotgun.

The bow of the boat bumped against the side of the barge. An outlaw stood at the head of the boat, gun in hand. He jumped on to the barge.

Slocum shot him from where he lay on his side on the deck. He'd finished reloading.

Parker grabbed the shotgun, holding it in both hands. He lay prone, raising up the weapon. He fired into the men on the boat at point-blank range. Then he gave them the other barrel.

Slocum came up on one knee and pumped lead into what was left of the men in the boat. Gunfire crackled after the two big booms of the shotgun. It was mostly a matter of finishing off, of delivering the coup de grace. He might have shot a dead man or two, but he wasn't taking any chances.

He squeezed the trigger until it clicked on an empty cylinder.

In the boat, nothing was moving, or even twitching.

One of Sutton's horses was thrashing in the water some twenty feet off the west end of the raft. During the fracas it had managed to break free and had trampled down the barrier gate and plunged into the river.

The other Sutton horse had broken through the decking and was stuck in place. Opposite, on the starboard side, Slocum's horse reared up, standing on two legs.

Slocum rose, holstering the empty gun. He went to his horse, not wanting to lose it. When its forelegs touched down, he grabbed the head harness and held the gray with all fours on the deck, gentling it. It didn't take much doing.

The horse wasn't that upset, more excited than anything else. The trader from whom Slocum had bought the horse had told him that the gray had come from a mining boom town, so it was used to gunfire and the smell of blood.

The horse in the water swam toward shore, coursing. On land, four mounted men rode back and forth, shouting and pointing at the barge.

One of them shot at the barge, and then they all did. They were shooting handguns, and none of the bullets came too close.

"Why, you sons of bitches," Slocum said, shucking his rifle out of its saddle sheath. He put it to his shoulder, pointed it at a rider, and fired, missing.

The riders popped off more shots, some plowing the water near the raft. Slocum made a slight hairline adjustment in his aiming and fired again, at the same man. This time he hit the target, knocking him from the saddle. He lay on the ground, alive, wounded.

One of his fellows swung down from the saddle, keeping the horse between him and the barge. Holding the reins in one hand, crouching, he made his way to the wounded man. Two other mounted men shot at Slocum.

The man on the ground had his hands full trying to hold a gun and the reins of his horse, while at the same time trying to reach the fallen man. The horse kept getting away from him, swinging its head to the outside, to the limit of the reins. He kept pulling it back hard, and it kept getting away from him.

The next time it pulled away, Slocum was ready for it. The horse reached the end of its tether, exposing the man. Slocum fired and the man went down, falling dead beside the wounded man. The reins slipped from dead hands and the horse ran away.

The other two had had enough. They wheeled the horses

around the wounded man, peppering the air with shots. One of them hopped down to the ground, to the wounded man. He got his hands under the wounded man's arms and lifted him to his feet, half-carrying and half-dragging him to the horse, which his mounted partner held in place.

When he lifted the wounded man up onto the animal's back, he'd be a perfect target. Slocum couldn't miss. He was pointing his rifle at the target when a hand reached out, pushing the weapon aside.

It was Clarissa Deane. "Please don't," she said. "They've had enough. They're running."

In the interval, the wounded man had been gotten up on the horse, and now his rescuer took hold of the saddlehorn and vaulted up into the saddle, snatching up the reins. With the wounded man holding onto him, the rider spurred his horse away from the shore, with his mounted companion riding beside him.

Slocum could have tagged one, maybe more, but Clarissa's hand was on the rifle, holding it down. Then the riders were over a ridge and safely away.

"Do you think they'd show any mercy to you? Or anyone else?" Slocum asked.

"I'm sorry," she said. "I know you must think me terribly weak, but to shoot men in the back when they're running away—well, it seems cold-blooded somehow, cruel. . . ."

"Not sporting enough for you, eh?"

"It sounds silly when you put it that way, but yes, in a way. . . . It lowers you to their level. It's something they would do."

Slocum shrugged. "What's done is done."

A cloud of gun smoke hung over the barge. Off the starboard side was the outlaws' boat, held in place by the current. Bodies were sprawled in the boat, some hanging over the side, in the water. A couple of bodies floated free, bobbing around the side of the barge.

The air smelled of cordite and blood.

Clarissa put a hand on Slocum's arm. "Please don't think me ungrateful. I hate to think of what would have happened if not for you. You're a very brave man."

"The preacher missed my extra gun, that's all," Slocum said.

Meachum, still drunk but sobering, said, "Damned funny preacher!"

Mack and Jack stood side by side, looking down at the body. Mack said, "Looks like somebody pried off the top of his head with a shovel and used it to scoop his brains out."

"Damned fine shooting," Jack said.

"Lucky shot," Slocum said.

"Not for him."

Slocum had meant to put the slug right between the preacher's eyes. Instead, he had shot three inches high—a killing shot, true, but still, he could do better.

"Parker's the hero," Slocum said. "He was ready to make a move on the preacher and he didn't even have a gun." That turned the others' attention to Parker and away from Slocum, which is what Slocum wanted.

Clarissa faced Parker, her eyes shining. "Yes, that was very brave of you, Mr. Parker!"

"Took a lot of sand," Mack said.

"Grit," said Jack.

"Shucks, guess I wasn't thinking," Parker said, laughing self-consciously.

Slocum said, "And it was Parker who really cleaned up on that bunch in the boat when he gave them both barrels of the scattergun."

"He sure did!" the elder Sutton said, his son nodding agreement.

"Damned fine work," Tiverton said, clapping Parker on the back.

Parker, pleased, said, "Good thing it was a shotgun. I can't hit a barn door with anything else! I just pointed the thing, closed my eyes, and let rip with both barrels.

"But *you*, mister, you sure showed some fancy gun work! Say, after all this, and I still don't know your name . . ."

"Slocum."

"Put 'er there, Mr. Slocum!" Parker stuck out his hand. Slocum shook it. Parker had a strong grip, but he didn't overdo it. He and Slocum smiled at each other.

"Glad to know you, Mr. Slocum." Parker looked around at the bodies. "Mighty glad!"

"Likewise. And just plain Slocum will do," he said.

Parker nodded. Looking as if he had just remembered something, he started feeling around the top of his head, his face registering comical surprise. "Hey, where's my hat? It must've fallen off."

He looked around. "There it is," somebody said, pointing at the derby, which lay on its side near the pulley-works.

"Fell off in all the excitement, I guess," Parker said, crossing to it. He leaned forward, reaching for it, making a clumsy misstep that caused him to kick the hat, sending it into the air.

"Whoops!" The hat skimmed across the deck, landing near the preacher's body. Parker squatted, picking it up. He brushed it off, then stuck a fist inside, knocking the dents out of the crown. He pulled it down on his head, tilted at a jaunty angle.

"This hat's seen me a long way. I'd hate to lose it now," he said, giving it a final pat on the crown.

Since the shooting had stopped, Tiny had been crouched over Big Joe, working on him. Now he looked up, saying, "I think he's coming around!"

Big Joe groaned. Tiverton said, marveling, "He must have a head as hard as an anvil!"

Tiny filled a bucket with river water and dashed it in Big Joe's face. Big Joe came awake, sputtering. He sat up too fast, cringing as the pain hit. He shrank, burying his head in his arms, crying, "Damn, that hurts!"

"I think he's going to be okay," Tiny said.

Big Joe gingerly felt around his head, exploring his aches and pains. The side of his face where he'd been kicked bore a scuffed boot mark. His jaw was swollen with an egg-sized lump, a big purple bruise, but it wasn't broken. He couldn't hear too well out of the ear that had been kicked.

"Wha—what happened?" he said thickly.

Tiny looked around, at a loss for words. He shrugged. Big Joe rubbed his eyes, his vision clearing, coming into focus. Then he saw the blood and the bodies.

"Yikes!" he said.

6

Sutton's horse swam ashore. It struggled out of the water onto dry land, shaky as a newborn colt. After it had gotten solid ground under all four hooves, it soon found its footing. It picked its way carefully through the stones of the riverbank. Its wet mane was plastered down, and water ran dripping from its sides. It shied away from the body on the shore, nickering. It ran away, but not too far, keeping to the near side of the ridgeline.

The two Suttons labored to free the horse that had broken through the deck planking. Mack and Jack gave them a hand. Soon the horse was standing safely foursquare on deck. Its forelegs had some nasty cuts, but nothing was broken.

Tiverton knelt beside the preacher, going through the dead man's pockets. He found his billfold and retrieved it. He kept turning out pockets, but came up empty.

"My watch—it's gone!" he said.

"Oh, that's too bad," Clarissa said.

"Hmmph," said Aunt Ethel, nodding grimly to herself.

Parker said, "It must've fallen out during the action."

"Hmmph," Aunt Ethel repeated.

Tiverton, peeved, said, "That watch is solid gold!"

"Maybe it didn't fall too far from the body," Parker said. "I'll help you look."

"I can look by myself," Tiverton snapped.

"Suit yourself," Parker said, shrugging.

Tiverton hunkered down, squatting beside the body. There was a lot of blood, but most of it was pooled by the preacher's head, where it made a red halo. Tiverton eyed the boards, square foot by square foot, looking for the gleam of gold, walking crouched down as he moved beside the body.

A shadow fell across him, making him look up. Slocum stood on the other side of the corpse, bending down to reach for something. Tiverton said, "Here now, what do you think you're doing?"

Slocum pulled the Colt out from where the preacher had stuck it in his waistband. "My gun," he said, rising, dropping the weapon into its holster.

Tiverton went back to looking for his watch. Parker said to Slocum, "Lucky thing, you having two guns."

"That was planning. Luck was him not finding the second gun," Slocum said.

"Well, you sure can shoot. Only other fellow I know who can handle a gun like that is Longbaugh."

"Longbaugh? Harry Longbaugh, the one they call the Sundance Kid?"

"I believe they do call him that sometimes," Parker said. "Know him?"

"Heard of him," Slocum said. "You?"

"No, no, I don't know the man, but I've seen him around a couple of times, in Laramie and Cheyenne. He's fast and accurate. Deadly accurate."

"Wyoming, that's nice country up there."

"Too much shooting. That's why I came south—figured it was safer," Parker said, grinning.

Tiverton announced, vexed, "I can't find my damned watch!"

"Too bad," Parker said. He offered helpfully, "Guess it must've fallen overboard."

Tiverton went back to looking, widening his search area. Slocum went to tend to his horse.

Aunt Ethel bumped into Parker, then gripped his arm. "Excuse me, Mr. Parker, I'm not so steady on my feet as I thought."

"That's okay, ma'am, I've got you."

Clarissa said, "Are you all right, Aunt Ethel?"

Aunt Ethel waved away her concerns. "I'm fine, dear. Mr. Parker kept me from stumbling."

"And now I'll do the same for you, Mr. Parker," she added in a voice so low that only she and Parker could hear it.

"Er, excuse me, ma'am?" Parker said guardedly.

"You played a hero's part today, Mr. Parker. It would be a shame to tarnish it," she went on, low-voiced.

He smiled, puzzled. "I don't follow you, ma'am."

"Tut-tut," she said. "I was watching you before, when you picked up your hat. The hat was not the only thing you picked up. Need I say more?"

"Well," Parker said. "I thought you might have been looking, but I didn't think your eyes were that good."

"You can't put one over so easily on an old Yankee like me. But at least you don't deny it."

"What now?"

"You've performed very creditably here, for the most part. Why spoil it with the name of *thief*?

"It would be well if Mr. Tiverton should find his watch," she added.

"I reckon so, ma'am."

Tiverton was on his hands and knees, some feet away from the body, scanning the deck. Mack and Jack hunkered down nearby. "What're you doing?" Tiverton asked.

"We're helping you look," Jack said.

"I said I don't need any help!"

Parker sidled over to the body, toeing it. He started, with a sudden show of great interest. He crouched, raising the corpse on one side and reaching under it.

"Hey, looky here," he said, pulling his hand out, holding a fistful of something gold.

Tiverton's head snapped around, homing in on the gleaming gold. "That's my watch!"

"That's right," Parker said, smiling. "It was lying under that rascal all the time."

"How about that!" Tiverton rose, unfolding his bony limbs, his face alight as he reached for his treasure. Parker dropped the gold watch and chain into his palm.

"Thanks!" Tiverton raised the timepiece's lid. "It's still ticking," he said. "Hasn't lost a second! Much obliged, young man, much obliged!" He shook Parker's hand, pumping it, slapping him on the back.

Mack muttered, "If I found it, I'd have kept it."

"He can afford it, the old skinflint," Jack said.

Hearing them, Tiverton turned and glared at them. "Fortunately, Mr. Parker is an honest man!" he said.

Parker smiled weakly.

Big Joe sat on the platform, holding his head and moaning, "My head, my head!"

Meachum brandished a pint bottle of whiskey that he'd found somewhere in his carpetbag. "Take a shot of this," he said.

Big Joe took a long pull from the bottle. He choked, his face reddening. "Gawd!"

Meachum pawed for the bottle. "If you don't want it, give it here."

"Who says I don't want it?" Big Joe demanded, fending off Meachum while taking another gulp.

He stood up shakily. Not all of his wobbling was due to the working over he'd gotten; some of it was bottle-bred. He staggered over to the corpse, looking down dumbly at it.

"I guess his head hurts even worse than mine," he said.

"Damned funny fellow! I don't think he was a preacher at all," Meachum said, reaching for the bottle.

7

Now that the shooting was done, with no sign of its immediate resumption, the regulars at the station came out to see what it was all about. Some of them piled into a longboat and pushed off from the landing, poling out to the barge. They brought a few jugs of whiskey along with them. The jugs were uncorked and passed around. That and the bodies floating around in the water created a kind of carnival-like air.

Big Joe wanted to go back to the dock, but the passengers wanted to go on. "We paid for a crossing," Tiverton said.

"You can have your money back," Big Joe said, which showed how much the stomping had sapped his vigor, since normally he'd never let so much as the smallest coin be pried from his clenching ham fists.

"We cross to the far bank," Slocum said. "This business isn't done yet." Big Joe hadn't seen what Slocum could do with a gun—he'd been unconscious when Slocum had made his move—but he'd heard enough about it in the short time he'd been awake to know that Slocum wasn't to be tangled with. It was easier to make the crossing than to cross him. Safer too.

With the help of those in the longboat, the barge crossed to the west bank. The rowboat with the dead outlaws inside it was towed alongside the barge, and grounded on shore. Some of the bodies floating loose in the river got away and drifted downstream.

The passengers cleared off the barge, stepping onto dry land. The longboat group joined them. Slocum eyed the dead outlaws, shaking his head. "I don't know them," he said. "Anybody here know any of these men?"

"Not me. I'm a stranger here myself," Parker said.

Big Joe glanced at the dead. "I don't know. A couple of 'em look kind of familiar, and then they don't. I might've seen them around before, and then again I might not, know what I mean?"

"That one there is Pete Polk," Tiny said, pointing at a white-faced, blue-jowled corpse.

"No, it ain't," Big Joe said, leaning forward for a better look. "Yes, it is, by Gawd! It is him. I didn't recognize him at first, he looks different dead, but that is him."

"Who's Pete Polk?" Slocum asked.

"A bad 'un, a real bad 'un," Tiny said, while some of the others nodded.

"He *was*," Tiny added, eyeing the body.

One of the men from the longboat spoke up. "He was a troublemaker and a mean drunk, one of that Black Diamond crowd."

Slocum turned to him. "Black Diamond? What's that?"

"There was a gang of claim jumpers and robbers who used to prey on the miners, before Dunbar and his bunch over to the Beefsteak Mines ran the bandits clear out of the canyon.

"Now they're all holed up at their hideout, the Black

Diamond ranch, in the hills. They come down from there whenever they feel like raising hell,'' the man from the longboat said.

"And this Polk was one of them?" Slocum asked.

The other nodded. "Not a big fish, but a medium-sized fish."

Somebody else said, "Some of these dead ones look like Black Diamond boys too."

A voice from back in the pack said, "You all talk too damn much."

The first one said, "Hell, what's Polk going to do about it now?"

"It ain't what he's going to do, it's what his friends who are still alive might do."

After that, nobody was too eager to offer any opinions about the Black Diamond bunch.

Slocum went to the outlaw he'd downed with the rifle. He was trailed by a handful of onlookers. The outlaw lay on his back, a hole in his chest. "Drilled dead center," Parker said.

If anyone knew who the dead man was, they didn't say. Slocum looked around, scanning the scene. "There's three of them. One wounded, and two on the same horse," he said. "That'll make them easier to track."

He climbed up on his horse and set out after them.

8

Reese fell off the horse again. He hit the ground with a grunt. The other times he'd fallen, he'd cried out, but this time he just grunted. Not even a groan, just grunted.

The horses stopped. There were two of them, ridden by the three men who'd escaped the big gunfight at the river crossing. Curly rode one horse, and Len and Reese shared the other, or at least they had until Reese had fallen off.

The horses stood, waiting patiently. They'd been ridden hard and were glad for the rest. The fugitives had fled northwest, angling across the valley into the hills. Anywhere else they would have been called mountains, but here in the Rockies they were only hills. Beyond them lay the real mountains, the lofty peaks of the Front Slope.

The hills hemmed in the landscape. Through them wound a trail, rising higher with each new turn. It was night, black and dark. The moon had not yet risen; the scene was lit by starlight. There was no other light and no sign of human habitation, had been none for miles.

Reese had been sitting behind Len, on the back of his horse, before he had fallen off. Now he lay on the ground, unmoving.

Curly was young and powerfully built. Len was homely with a big nose.

Curly said, "Damn."

Len said, "Reese! Reese, you all right?"

No reply.

"Damn!" Curly said feelingly. He and Len spoke low-voiced, though as far as they knew, there was no one else around—except Reese, of course. But the lonesome night trail discouraged loudness.

Len got down from his horse. He was stiff from hours of hard riding. He let the reins fall. The horse stayed in place, tired.

Len looked back along the trail, the way they had come. In the starlight, it was a pale ribbon spilling downward into the rocks.

"Anybody following?" Curly asked.

"No," Len said, "not that I could see them if there was." His spurs jingled as he went around the horse to Reese and crouched down beside him.

Reese lay curled on his side, an older man, scruffily bearded. His shirt was soaked in blood. He'd been shot in the back, under his left shoulder wing. Under his shirt was the bulge of some makeshift bandaging, a hasty attempt to patch him up so he wouldn't bleed to death. His face was stiff, white. His eyes were closed.

Curly said, "He dead?"

"I can hear him breathing," Len said after a pause. Curly made a noise that might have meant disgust, or maybe he was just clearing his throat.

"He's wheezing, kind of. Making a bubbling noise," Len said.

"Shot through the lung maybe. Probably. Well, what do we do now?"

"Get him back on the horse. Climb down and give me a hand."

Curly stayed put in the saddle. "He can't sit no horse. Hell, he's out."

Len shook Reese's shoulder, calling his name. He didn't shake too hard because he was afraid that would start the bleeding again. Reese's breathing deepened, but that was all.

"If he can't ride on the horse, he can ride across it," Len said.

Curly snorted. "That'll finish him off."

"We're not so far from the ranch. He'll make it."

"We still haven't reached the pass, and the ranch is a couple miles past that."

"What else can we do?" Len asked. Curly said nothing. Len said, "Well?"

Curly stared off into space, looking at the stars. He kept tapping the ends of the reins against the saddle, irritated, impatient.

"How about it, Curly?"

"Damn," Curly said, stepping down. He went to Len and stood beside him. Len crouched over Reese, reaching for him. "If we each get him by an arm, we can lift him up—"

Reese grabbed him instead, his hand clutching convulsively at Len's forearm. At the same instant, his eyes popped open, haunted, staring. It gave Len quite a start. He stiffened, gasping.

"Len! Len!" Reese bawled out loudly, his voice a harsh croak. Len flinched from the force of it.

He said, "Easy, Reese."

"Tell him to shut the hell up," Curly muttered loud enough to be heard by Reese.

"Help me so I can sit up," Reese said. The others lifted him so that he was sitting with his back propped up by a rock. The effort left him exhausted, and it was some minutes before he had recovered sufficiently to talk.

He said, "I can't ride, it'll kill me. That slug tore me up pretty good inside. I ain't got much left, boys."

"You'll be okay once we get to the ranch," Len said.

Curly pointedly looked away, up the trail. Never once looking at Reese, he said, "We'll ride on ahead and come back with the others."

Reese's hand shot out, once again gripping Len's arm. "Don't leave me!"

Len pried the fingers off his arm, flexing it. It was numb where Reese had held it. "Nothing wrong with your grip," Len said, a little sulky.

"Don't leave me alone," Reese pleaded. "Let Curly go on ahead and you stay with me. That way I know somebody'll come back for me."

"That's crazy talk! What do you think we're going to do, leave you out here?" Len asked, indignant.

"You wouldn't," Reese said, putting the accent on the "you."

"You're damned right I wouldn't, and neither would Curly."

"You wouldn't run out on a pal?"

"Hell, no!"

Curly put his hands on his hips, still looking up the trail. Reese spoke to Len, saying, "I can make it, all I need is a rest!"

"Sure," Len said soothingly.

Curly said, "One of us should go, Len."

"You go."

"You go. Stay or go, it's all the same to me, so long as one of us gets moving. I'll stay."

"No!" Reese said. "You go, Curly."

"If that's how you feel about it . . ."

"I do."

Curly turned to Len. "Your call."

Len was frustrated at the way he was being trapped. He didn't want to stay either, but he couldn't wriggle out of it now without looking like a skunk.

"Stay," Reese said.

"I'll stay," Len said at last, sighing.

Curly said, "You sure?"

"Yes. You go to the ranch. They can rig up some kind of litter or stretcher to fetch Reese back with," Len said.

"Okay." Curly went to his horse, mounting up. "I'll be going then," he said.

"Hurry back," said Len.

"It's gonna take a couple of hours."

"We'll be here."

Curly rode off, starting up the trail. It was the same starlit ribbon, but this time it was slanting upwards. The horse clopped up the trail and away.

Reese spat. "He couldn't get out of here fast enough. He's yellow." He laughed. It sounded like gargling. "Who am I to judge? I showed yellow myself.

"I don't back off from no man. You know that."

"I know it," Len said. Tactfully left unmentioned was the fact that they had backed off from the gunfight at the crossing.

"You can fight a man, but you can't fight the high country," Reese went on. "All them rocks constantly hanging over on you, crushing you down, going up and up and up . . .

"They make a man feel small, like a bug. It's worse at night, in the dark," Reese said, shuddering. "Just thinking about being left alone out here made me feel like I was drowning.

"That's why I showed yellow. You understand, don't you, Len?"

"Sure," Len said, uncomfortable. "You don't have to talk about it if you don't want to."

"I want to. It helps to talk."

"It don't help to keep making that spook talk. Like a couple of kids scaring themselves in the dark."

"Don't get sore, Len, I was just talking," Reese said. "You're a real friend. That's why I wanted you to stay. I knew I could trust you.

"Curly would've waited around long enough to make it look good. Then he would've rode off and caught up to you and told you I was dead. If I lived, he could've said that he made a mistake, that he just thought I was dead."

"You think you got Curly figured pretty good, don't you?"

"Don't you?" Reese countered.

"He's been a pretty good friend to you."

"Sure, when things were going good. Now he's scared, like me, and he doesn't have the sand to stay out on the trail at night, with only a wounded man for company."

"Can't imagine why not," Len said tightly.

"Don't be hard on me. I'm hurting."

Len picked up a pebble and threw it. "Forget it." After a while, Reese laughed and Len asked him what was so funny.

"Curly." Reese laughed again, a mean laugh, but weak. Not that weak, though. "I was just thinking that I wouldn't want to be the one to have to break the news to Gus about how our bunch got hit down at the crossing."

"No, Gus won't like that," Len said.

"It ain't safe sometimes to be the bearer of bad news."

"Not to Gus."

They both fell silent, and for the next few minutes, the only sounds were Reese's heavy breathing and the occasional movements of Len's horse. Reese's breathing sounded like air being sucked through a wet rag.

The trail was a dry streambed running down the middle of a ravine. On either side, wooded slopes rose to rocky cliffs hundreds of feet high. The slopes were thickly forested with pine. The ravine floor was chock-full of rocks, pony-sized, wagon-sized, house-sized. Thrusting out of the rockpile at odd angles were fallen dead trees, whole trees, twenty and thirty feet long, complete with snaky branches and roots.

Overhead was a starry sky. The night was crisp and cool. Not frosty, but cold, especially so to those who sat and waited. The ravine was sheltered from the wind, but it was still cold.

"I'm cold," Reese said. Len unrolled his bedroll and covered him with it. Time passed—how much was difficult to say. A lot less than he thought was Len's unhappy conviction.

More time passed, the stars remaining fixed and immobile in the sky. Reese sat on the ground, which was cushioned by dead pine needles. He huddled in the blanket, propped up against a smooth-faced boulder. Opposite sat Len, facing him. Nearby stood the horse, tied to a tree.

Reese said, "How about a fire?"

"Better not," Len said. "It could be seen a long way off."

"It'll guide the others to us."

"Maybe they won't be our boys."

Reese started, suddenly uneasy. "Who else would it be?"

"I don't know."

"Think we're being chased?"

"No," Len said. That wasn't entirely true. Earlier, in daylight, he'd had the feeling that they were being followed. A couple of times, he thought he'd seen a moving blur behind them, far away, at the very edge of visibility. He wasn't sure of what he'd seen, or if he'd seen anything at all, so he hadn't sounded off about it. A posse would have raised a cloud of dust, and there hadn't been any so it wasn't a posse. But he had glimpsed that crawling antlike blur in the distance more times than he'd cared to. Then the sun had gone down and there was no seeing it whether it was there or not, so he'd put it out of his mind. Until now.

He kept his mouth shut about it. No sense getting Reese any more stirred up than he already was.

Reese said, "Nobody'd come after us this close to Black Diamond canyon, they don't have the guts."

"The law wouldn't," Len said. "It's not worth their while to come stir up a hornet's nest. But the railroad men will."

"Colonel Deane will. We made a try for his daughter. He ain't gonna forget or forgive, not as long as he's alive."

"Then he won't live long."

"I don't know, he's a tough old bird," Len said doubtfully.

"He can't have gotten after us so soon," Reese said. "Light a fire, will you?"

Len sighed. "Reese . . ."

Reese's teeth chattered. "Just a small fire."

"A small fire can be seen a long way off."

"I'm so cold I'm turning numb. Please."

"Hell," Len said, rising. He gathered up handfuls of dry pine needles and armfuls of dead branches. He built a small fire in a circle of stones between him and Reese. The dry pine needles made good kindling, and soon the teepee of twigs was ablaze with hot yellow flames. Len piled on more branches, feeding the fire. Wood popped and crackled, burning.

A cone of yellow-orange firelight blossomed in the ravine's black darkness.

"Thanks," Reese said, basking in the cheery warmth.

Time passed, the firewood dwindling to a few scant sticks. Len got up and gathered more firewood.

"The boys are taking a long time getting here," Reese said.

"It's a couple hours ride, there and back," Len said. "Curly's probably getting there just about now."

"No! You reckon?" Reese asked, disappointed. Len didn't say anything. He fed another stick to the fire.

The moon came up, turning the sky purple-blue, with milky washes of light glowing down the star lanes.

Hours passed. The fire had burned down to dim embers. The ravine was locked down in the heart of the night. A bird sounded in the trees, not chirping, but making a kind of cawing noise. A plaintive, slightly mournful cry, like a series of low notes sounded on a woodwind instrument.

It called out and fell silent. There was no reply, and the night bird did not sound again.

Reese said, "God! What's keeping 'em? I'm freezing to death!

"Len! You hear me, Len? You awake?"

"Yes," Len said. He sat hunched deep in his coat, hat pulled down.

"I drifted off. What time is it?"

"Late."

"They should've been here by now."

"I wish to hell they were," Len said harshly. Reese didn't say anything for a while.

"Len, the fire's gone out."

"I noticed," Len said dryly.

"Can you get it going again?"

"No."

"Why not?"

"I'm out of matches."

Reese stirred. "You've got more, I saw them!"

"I'm out of firewood then."

"You'll have to get more."

"Get it yourself."

"Len! I can't! I'm shot!"

"Hold your horses, I'll get it going after a while."

"But you will do it." Reese settled back, groaning.

"Later."

"I'm awful cold, Len. I'm going numb."

"Shut up." After a long silence, Len rose, saying, "All right, dammit."

His legs were cold and stiff. All of him was. He stomped around, trying to get some feeling in his feet. He rubbed his hands together, blowing on them.

"I hear something," he said, suddenly alert. High up on the trail, hoofbeats sounded. A small rock was dislodged and rolled downhill, striking other rocks, setting off a series of sharp clicks that sounded like billiard balls in collision.

The moon was almost directly overhead, shining down into the ravine. At the top of the trail, a rider swung into view, a black outline against the sky.

The rider started down the trail, followed by another rider, and another, until a line of them came creeping downhill. They came at a deliberate pace, a mountain trail at night being no place for hurrying.

"It's them!" Reese cried.

The riders came to the flat place in the ravine floor where Len and Reese waited. There were about a dozen riders in all, a hard-bitten crew of gunmen and killers, the Black Diamond crowd.

They grouped their horses in a semicircle, facing Len and Reese. They did not dismount. They were silent, their faces hard, unfriendly.

At their head was Gus Andrews, a six-and-a-half-foot-tall Texan, the boss of the bunch. With his high-crowned hat he topped seven feet. He had a square-shaped face, dark eyes, and a walrus mustache. His horse was huge, an over-sized charger that would have looked at home pulling a beer wagon.

Len and Reese were silent, sensing trouble. Gus was flanked by his trusted sidemen, Silverado and Charlie Pye. Silverado was a lean young gun. Charlie Pye was full-blown and whiskery.

Silverado indicated Len and Reese with a nod of his head. "Two of them, just like Curly said. So he wasn't lying about that."

"Bring him here," Gus said.

A gap opened in the line of horsemen, making room for Curly, who was brought up from the back of the pack. His horse's reins were held by Charlie Pye.

Curly sat shrunken in the saddle, holding onto the horn with both hands. His face was swollen and purple, a mass of bruises. He had been brutally beaten. One eye was swollen shut; the other was a slit that he squinted out of. He started crying when he was led to the front, sobbing softly.

The sound of those sobs froze Len's blood. Reese said, "God, his face!"

"What—what happened?" Len asked.

"He told me a cock-and-bull story about how the girl got away, and I didn't believe him," Gus said. He sounded mildly interested, as if he was discussing the price of beef in Kansas.

Curly sobbed unbrokenly. Gus said, "Charlie."

Charlie Pye leaned over in the saddle, reaching for Curly. Curly flinched, crying out.

"Bless your soul, I ain't gonna hurt you no more," Charlie Pye said, chuckling. He patted Curly's heaving shoulders. "Hush now," he said.

Gus said, "What happened at the crossing, Len? You might want to think a minute before giving me the same story as Curly."

Len swallowed, then found his voice, strong and sure. "I don't know what he told you. I only know the truth."

"And what's that?"

"We got the shit shot out of us."

Someone in the gang snickered. Silverado looked around to see who it was, but by then the snickering had stopped. Gus hadn't so much as cracked a smile.

"How could that be? You had nine good guns and an inside man," he said.

"I don't know. The preacher must've slipped up. He was the first to die," Len said. "After that, the barge opened up on the boys. Shot 'em to pieces."

"It's true," Reese chimed in. "There must've been a half-dozen shooters hidden on board, maybe more."

"Nobody asked you," Silverado said.

Gus motioned for Len to continue. Len said, "The only thing I can figure is that somehow they knew we were coming and they were ready for us."

Gus scowled, shaking his head. "Colonel Deane wouldn't use his own daughter as ambush bait."

"If it was her. Maybe they used a decoy."

"I heard different, and the one who told me was close enough to the colonel to know."

"Well, something went wrong," Len said defiantly.

"I reckon," Gus said.

Charley Pye said, "What do you think, Gus?"

"Len ain't no bullshitter. Maybe it happened like Curly said."

"Aw, you mean we beat up this poor fellow for nothing?"

"He had it coming," Silverado said. "He's a yellow bastard anyhow."

"I tol' you I wasn't lyin'," Curly mouthed through smashed lips.

"Hush," Charlie Pye soothed.

"It's a bad business," Gus said. "Whatever happened, our side got a bloody nose. If I thought somebody tipped the colonel off . . ." He left that thought unfinished.

He said, "Mount up, Len."

Reese said, "What about me?"

"Right. Finish him off, Len."

Len, crossing to his horse, paused in mid-stride. He turned and stared Gus in the face. He said, "What?"

"Reese. He's no good to us. Kill him," Gus said.

"No, no!" Reese cried.

"You got sand, Len. These other two ain't worth spit. At least I think you got sand. You can prove it by shooting Reese."

"Don't kill me!"

"I ain't gonna kill you," Len said.

Gus drew his gun and shot Reese. A puff of smoke clung to his gun. The report echoed through the ravine.

Len looked at Reese. He sat slumped with his chin on his chest, shot through the heart. Len looked at Gus, then went for his gun. "Dirty murdering bastard—"

Silverado shot him dead. Gus said, "Make it a clean sweep."

Charlie Pye pushed Curly off his horse and shot him on

the ground. Gus turned his horse so that he faced the rest of his men.

"They fucked up," he said, meaning the dead men. "Don't fuck up."

9

Gus and his men took the two riderless horses in tow and rode off, back the way they came.

Slocum watched them go. He was hiding in a pine thicket on a low rise overlooking the floor of the ravine. He'd been hiding there for a long time, since before the arrival of Gus and his men. He'd been tracking the three fugitives all day. It was easy—three men on two horses, with one of the men hit and badly wounded. All he'd had to do was follow the blood trail until he came in sight of them. After that, he'd kept well back, dogging them. When the sun had gone down, he'd closed the distance. When Len and Reese had halted while Curly went on ahead, Slocum had tethered his horse in a wooded glade off the trail, and gone the rest of the way on foot, creeping through the rocks and trees. He could have taken the two men any time he wanted, but instead he had hunkered down in his hiding place and waited. So he'd seen and heard all that had happened.

He rose, stiff and cold from staying in one place for so long. He stepped out of the edge of the woods, into the open. He brushed a mass of dead pine needles off his front.

"Gus," he said. He knew Gus, knew him from the old

days. There was no way he was going to trail Gus into the depths of his mountain fastness. Slocum had done enough for one night. Besides, the location of Black Diamond canyon was no secret. Everyone knew where it was. Riding into it and getting out alive was what was hard.

Slocum went back to his horse and followed the moonlit trail south, out of the ravine. In the trees a lone night bird piped a mournful call.

10

Slocum made sure he was off the Black Diamond trail and a damned sight away from it before he pitched camp for what remained of the night. He did not light a fire.

He awoke before dawn. He'd had enough of beef jerky and campfire coffee. He rode off to town to get a real breakfast.

Mountain Valley Junction was the town. Mountain Valley was a long high-country valley, what was called in these parts a park. It ran north-south, bordered on the west by a mountain range, and on the east by the river. Black Diamond Canyon was in the hills northwest of the park. Mountain Valley Junction was at the midpoint, sitting astride the mouth of Spanish Pass, a major gateway through the western mountains. One of the pass's branches was Lonesome Canyon, site of the Beefsteak gold mine.

Slocum came down on the town from the west. The sky was light, but the sun had not yet risen. It was a colorless sky. The hills were ringed with deep blue shadows. There was dew on the grass and the flatland was covered with mist. The town rose out of the mist like an island.

The main body of the town consisted of a courthouse

square and a few hotels, stores, eateries, and all the rest. That was the old town, which had existed in more or less its present form since the territory had been acquired by the United States, and had grown more recently since the granting of statehood to Colorado.

South of it was the boom town that had sprung up almost literally overnight, after gold was first struck in Lonesome Canyon. It had been a roaring camp of whores, whiskey, and gamblers, with a killing or two every night. It had subsided when the miners led by Dunbar had cracked down, cleaning out the worst element. But the coming of the railroads had lit a fire under the kettle yet again, and now it was fast coming to a boil.

Both parts of town were quiet enough as Slocum neared, except for a bare patch of ground on the outskirts where a pack of skinny dogs yelped and nipped at each other.

He angled toward the main town. The dogs yipped and snarled at him, crouching low to the ground.

"I'll shoot your ass," Slocum said pleasantly. The dogs started barking, lunging toward his horse, then stopping short.

"I mean it," he said, putting a hand on his gun. The dogs turned and ran away. "You know about guns, eh?" Slocum said, half-smiling.

There was movement in the streets, people awake and about. This was a country of early risers and it was well past first light. A small cafe on a side street a few blocks west of the town square looked clean and not too crowded. Slocum tied his horse to the hitching post and went inside.

There were about a half-dozen tables, mostly filled. The diners were mostly townsmen, the railroad men and miners being already at work at their out-of-town sites.

Some of the diners looked up when Slocum came in, not being obvious about it, but eyeing him, checking him out for a few seconds before returning to their breakfasts. None met his eye or looked at him for too long.

He sat down at a small table on the side, facing the door. Now he could see who came in. Behind him, at the back of the room, was the kitchen. There was the smell of frying grease and hot coffee, the sound of something sizzling on the griddle.

A girl came out to take his order. She was young, strong, well scrubbed, and cheerful. A basket of biscuits and a pot of strong black coffee were set out on his table straightaway, while his food was cooking. That took the edge off his hunger and stopped his stomach from rumbling until breakfast was served.

It was a big plateful of steak and eggs and fried potatoes. He wolfed it down, mopping up the eggs with still-warm biscuits.

Another pot of coffee would just about do it. He looked around for the girl, glancing over his shoulder. She stood in the mouth of the passageway leading back to the kitchen. Beside her stood a handsome redheaded woman. The two were in close conversation.

He caught the girl's eye. She crossed to his table, while the redheaded woman stepped back, out of sight. Too bad. She was a fine-looking woman.

Slocum took his time with the second pot of coffee, savoring it. He leaned back in his chair, pleasantly full. Diners at a couple of tables finished up, paid up, and went out.

The redheaded woman was back. She stood nearby, a hand on one hip, studying him. She was good-looking in a hard way. He nodded politely to her. She crossed to his table.

He pushed back his chair, starting to rise. "Don't get up," she said, so he sat. She had brick-red hair tied up in a prim knot at the top of her head, large green eyes, and a full ripe mouth that was held in a tight straight line. Her features were chiseled, clean-lined but cold.

She was tall, straight-backed, high-breasted, and leggy. She was buttoned up from the neck down in a severe dark shirt-dress with a hem that reached below the ankles. She stood with her hands folded across her chest.

She said, "Something I can do for you, mister?"

He shrugged. "The way you were looking at me, I thought you might know me."

Her mouth twisted in a cynical half-smile. "I know the type."

"What type is that?"

"Gunman," she said.

He shrugged again.

"You look a little more intelligent than most of them," she said, "and you're no kid, so you must know something to have lived this long."

She put her hands on her hips, glaring down at him, hot-eyed. The rest of her cool creamy face was immobile.

"Think you're man enough for the job?" she asked challengingly.

"What job is that, ma'am?"

She scowled. "Don't play games with me, cowboy."

He shook his head, honestly puzzled. "I think maybe you've got me mistaken for somebody else, ma'am."

Doubt showed on her face. "Wait a minute. Who are you?"

"The name's Slocum."

"You know who I am?"

"Uh, no."

That irked her a little, stinging her on her pride. "I'm Eileen Barrett."

"Glad to know you."

She looked at him like he was an idiot. "Eileen Barrett?

That name means nothing to you?'' She searched his face for some sign of recognition, finding none.

''No, ma'am. Sorry.''

''Then you haven't come to try for the reward?''

''No. What reward?''

She drew into herself, her cheeks coloring. ''Never mind. You're right, I must have mistaken you for somebody else.''

''That's one way to get acquainted,'' he said.

She'd started to turn away, but now she turned back to face him again, with those same coolly appraising eyes and that cynical half-twist to her mouth.

''Is your gun for hire?'' she asked.

''I'm a peace-loving man.''

''That's no answer. I had you figured right from the start. You're a gunman.''

He didn't deny it. She looked more interested. ''New in town?'' she asked.

''Just got in.''

She smiled to herself, as if some private thought had just been confirmed. ''That explains it. Well, you came to the right place. There's plenty of gun work to be had here in the junction.''

''That reward you mentioned sounds kind of interesting,'' he prompted.

''You don't know the half of it,'' she said. ''After you've got your bearings, come around some night and I'll tell you about it. If you live.''

''I'll do that.''

''Don't get yourself into a lather before you find out what it's all about, cowboy.''

''I won't, ma'am. I'm real careful,'' he said, but he was talking to her retreating back, for she had already turned and started toward the rear passage. She disappeared into it, not looking back.

Slocum, bemused, finished off his coffee. Eileen Barrett did not return. The girl came to his table to see if he wanted anything else.

"Just the bill," he said. "That redheaded woman—"

"That's Miz Barrett, the owner," she said.

"Interesting lady."

The girl smirked. "You'll find out."

"Is that so bad?"

The girl looked around to make sure no one else was listening. As she bent over to clear his place, she said, "They don't call her the Red Widow for nothing!"

Another table's order came up, and she bustled away to serve them before she could expand on her remark. Things got busy in the cafe, and the time for confidences went past.

Slocum settled the bill, left a tip, and went out, thoughtful.

Red Widow, eh?

11

Oliver Crabshaw was white-haired and gray-bearded, with reddish-pink skin and blue eyes, a small man in dirty buckskins. He wore his hat with the brim pinned up in front mule-skinner-style. He wore a big gun on his hip, a veritable hand cannon.

He was at the reins of a four-horse team pulling a supply wagon laden with crates and sacks. He was heading out of town when he saw Slocum.

Slocum had just come out of the cafe, and was standing on the corner of the raised wooden plank sidewalk that fronted the block. He was thoughtful, scratching his head. With half an eye he was watching the town go about its business around him.

The wagon rolled past. He glanced at the driver, then held the glance, recognizing him. He and the driver looked at each other. The driver had a delayed reaction. After a few beats, he gave a fair imitation of a man who'd been struck by lightning, sitting bolt upright in his seat, goggling.

He hauled in on the reins, jerking them up sharp, causing the team to come to a sudden halt. "Thunderation! If it ain't my old pal Slocum," he said.

Slocum flipped him a quick two-finger salute. "Hello, Crabby."

"Damn me if you ain't a sight for sore eyes! The bad penny always turns up, eh?"

"Meaning you or meaning me?" Slocum asked pointedly.

"Both!"

A couple of riders coming along the street had to swing wide to get around the stalled wagon. They gave Crabshaw dirty looks, which he ignored.

He leaned over the edge of the seat at the front of the wagon. "That sure was some turkey shoot you had down by the river!"

"Like it?"

"Whoo-whee, the feathers flew!" Crabshaw leered with lip-smacking relish. "When I seen them jaspers all laid out dead along the riverbank, like a string of fresh-caught fish, and I heard you done it, I said, 'That's my boy!' "

"Not so loud. Pipe down, will you?"

Crabshaw started. Dawning comprehension showed on his face, followed by a big wink. "Don't want to tip your hand just yet, huh?"

"If the dead men had any friends, I'd just as soon not meet them until I've had time to digest my breakfast," Slocum said.

"Dead bad men ain't got no friends."

"You never know, Crabby. Somebody might want to even up for yesterday."

"I get you. Okay, mum's the word. You can count on me to keep my mouth shut."

"I'm sure," Slocum said dryly. "But what're you doing in these parts, Crabby?"

"I'm working for the railroad. Red Rock, Colonel Deane's outfit. I just come up to pick up these here supplies, and I'm headed back to End of Track.''

''The colonel there?''

''I reckon. You know him, he's the first there in the morning, and the last to leave at night.''

''Hmmm. Think I might just head out that way myself.''

''Well, hop on and ride with me. We can catch up on old times.''

''All right,'' Slocum said. He hitched his horse to the back of the wagon and climbed up on the front seat beside Crabshaw.

Two men swung around a corner and into view, walking side by side in the street. They were big and tough-looking, and wore guns and badges.

The burlier of the two said, ''Something wrong with the wagon?''

''Nope,'' Crabshaw said.

''Then move it, you're blocking the road.'' He wasn't unfriendly, but he wasn't overly warm either.

''Yessir.'' Crabshaw gathered up the reins, urging the team forward. The wagon lurched, then rolled out of town. The two lawmen stood in the street, watching it go.

When the wagon had gone fifty feet, Slocum looked back. The duo still stood in the road, watching him. After a hundred feet or so, they moved on, going elsewhere.

Crabshaw nudged Slocum with an elbow. ''They wouldn't have been so high-and-mighty if they'd've knowed who was setting up here beside me,'' he said, sly-eyed and cackling.

''That's the kind of thing I'm trying to avoid.''

''You're mellowing in your old age, Slocum.''

''Mellow, hell! Who's the law in town?'' he asked.

''Mitch Mittelgard,'' Crabshaw said.

''Never heard of him.''

''Mitt, they call him, on account of he's always got his

mitt out, looking for somebody to put some dollars in it. At least he's fair. He takes from everybody and don't play no favorites.''

''Those deputies looked like they could handle themselves.''

''They can. There's five of them, plus Mitt, hardcases everyone of them. If they wasn't, the gangs would've torn down the town a long time ago.

''You see, the town pays Mitt. The respectable folk, the businessmen. They know that when the railroad comes through, there's going to be a lot of money to be made, and they aim to be around to make it. And they want him to crack down on Boom Town, keep the trouble south of the deadline,'' Crabshaw said.

The deadline was the imaginary line marking the boundary between the town proper and the anything-goes Boom Town district.

''Cut up in town, and Mitt and the boys'll come down on you like the wrath of God,'' Crabshaw explained. ''But it's mostly hands-off Boom Town, and he don't lift a finger for nothing that happens outside the town limits.''

''Who's he backing, Sovereign or Red Rock?'' Slocum asked.

''He don't say.'' Crabshaw glanced shrewdly at Slocum, saying, ''Like most folks in town, he's sitting on the fence, waiting to see who comes out on top. ''That's good, though, in a way. It means he don't favor one side over t'other when there's a squall.''

The town was left behind as the wagon rolled west along a well-rutted dirt road. The land was more or less level, but by no means flat, with plenty of dips and rises, streams and stands of timber.

Slocum said, ''Got anything to cut the dust?''

From a belt pouch, Crabshaw pulled out a pint of red liquor. "You know me!"

"That's why I asked." Slocum took the bottle, uncorking it with his teeth. The fumes stung his nose and made his eyes water. He took a swallow.

His face reddened, swelling as if under pressure. He coughed, wheezing.

"Good, huh?" Crabshaw asked.

"God, no! It's terrible!"

"Well, give it here, then. I'll find a use for it."

Slocum fended him off with one hand while taking another pull from the bottle. Again he was seized by a violent reaction. While he was recovering, Crabshaw took advantage of his weakened condition, prying the bottle from his hand.

The red whiskey was more than half gone. "Thunderation! I'd hate to see what was left if it warn't terrible," Crabshaw said. He took his turn, and then there was none.

"You do pretty good for yourself there, old-timer," Slocum said.

They rode on. The sun had burned off the morning mists. The sky was clear and blue, the meadows green. The air was fresh and clear.

Slocum said, "What do you know about this Eileen Barrett, the redheaded woman who runs the cafe?"

Crabshaw looked at him sideways. "You sure ain't been wasting no time."

"Strange woman."

"She's good-looking—and dangerous."

"All good-looking women are dangerous." After a pause, Slocum added, "All women are dangerous. And all men."

"Some more than others. Her in particular. She keeps the graves filled in Boot Hill."

"A nice lady like that? Well, not nice—strange is more like it—but she's no killer."

"Not directly," Crabshaw said. "She don't pull the trigger on 'em, but the result is the same as if she had."

"The Red Widow, eh?"

"They do call her that."

"That's what I'm told," Slocum said.

"Well, it's the truth," said Crabshaw. "Not that she's so bad, but she's got murder on her mind and she don't care who gets buried along the way."

Slocum glanced at him curiously. "What's her story?"

"A simple tale. Her husband was gunned down by an outlaw. It was murder, but they was both packing guns, so the law couldn't do nothing about it and the killer got away with it."

"Who was he? The killer, I mean."

"A piece of poison named Silverado, a backshooting polecat."

"He shoots pretty good from the front too," Slocum said.

Crabshaw looked surprised. "You know him?"

"I've seen him around."

"I thought you said you just got here," Crabshaw said, suspicious.

"I've been busy."

"I reckon! You sure do get around, son. Not that I much approve of some of the company you've been keeping."

"I saw him, he didn't see me."

"Oh, is that it? Been dogging him already, have you?" Crabshaw shook his head. "That redheaded woman must've had a powerful effect on you!"

"It was something else, didn't have anything to do with her," Slocum said. "So Silverado killed her man, huh? Interesting."

"It gets better. You see, she wants to get Silverado so bad that she's sworn to give herself to the man who kills him."

Slocum stared at Crabshaw. "The hell you say!"

"May lightning strike me if I'm lying," Crabshaw said, piously looking up. The sky remained a clear bright blue.

"Guess that shows you," he said after a pause.

"I still don't believe it. Where'd you hear that?" Slocum asked.

"It's common knowledge."

"Oh, sure."

"It's a well-known fact! It ain't no secret. Ask her, she'll tell you."

"If that doesn't beat all," Slocum said.

"You know how many have tried?" Crabshaw held up a hand, with the thumb down and the four fingers sticking up. "*Four*. Four men have tried, good guns every one. But none as good as Silverado, and that's why there's four graves grouped together on Boot Hill. The widow puts fresh flowers on 'em every Sunday.

"Silverado thinks it's funny, or at least he claims to. He must be laughing, 'cause he's burned down every man that came up against him. He's a snake, and he's fast as one too."

Slocum was unconvinced. "I'd as soon shoot him down as not, just on general principles. And that's without that fine woman being tossed into the bargain."

"She ain't ugly," Crabshaw said. "Folks have been wondering who the fifth man was going to be."

"What matters is who's in the fifth grave."

"Huh! Maybe Silverado won't think it's so goddamn funny any more."

"Don't go shouting it from the rooftops. I'd like it to be a surprise if I try for him."

"Wild horses couldn't get it out of me," Crabshaw assured him.

"Anyway, that's just a sideline. That redhead is strictly for dessert."

"My, Mr. Slocum, how you do talk! Watch out that she's not too spicy for you."

Slocum gave him a look that said he could take care of himself.

They neared the west end of the park, which opened on Spanish Pass, a tremendous multi-branched maze of passages and canyons winding through the mountains. The mouth of the pass was a couple of miles across. The ends were enclosed by tall cliffs.

The wagon crested the top of a ridge, Crabshaw reining the team to a halt, the wheels kicking up dust. Below lay a panoramic view of the pass and the surrounding area for miles around.

There was a line of dust in the north and a line of dust in the south. Both lines were driving toward the pass, which lay between them. Both were still several miles from their goal.

The sun was still low, its slanting rays picking out the dust clouds and making them stand out. In the early morning light they looked golden. They ran north-south. At their bases were what looked like giant fuzzy black caterpillars inching their way across the landscape.

In reality they were work crews, railroad work crews. There were pickmen and shovel men, rock-breakers, graders, and tracklaying gangs. Hundreds of men in both groups, leagued into twin rival organisms whose sole purpose was to extend their respective railroad lines as fast and as far as possible.

"That's the Sovereign line in the north, and the Red

Rock in the south,'' Crabshaw said. ''Whichever one gets to Lonesome Canyon first wins the race.''

''Looks like they're closing in on the home stretch,'' Slocum said.

''They're laying track at the rate of a couple of miles a day. Pretty soon they'll be within rifle range of each other.''

''That bad, huh?''

''Mister, you couldn't have come at a better time.''

''Good,'' Slocum said.

12

End of Track, the end of the line. The furthermost extension of the railroad. For the Red Rock Railroad, on this particular day, that point had been reached a few miles below the south gate of the pass. The tracks stretched south across the valley, following a sweeping curve that turned east, crossing the river and ultimately connecting with the hub at Manitou Springs.

At End of Track, the line was constantly extending itself. Beyond where the rails ended, the road had been surveyed, bedded, and graded. Cross-timbers were laid down, rails were laid across them at right angles and hammered into place, and then the crews moved on to the next section, repeating the process. Length by length the road drove north.

It was a scene of intense activity. The tracklaying crews made up a multi-armed human machine, setting up a constant din. Its efforts raised the dust clouds.

Not far behind, further down the line, stood a supply train, its flatbed cars piled high with rails and wooden ties, crates of tools, and barrels of iron spikes. The cargo was being loaded onto wagons, which ferried it up the line.

Near the train, the tracks branched off onto a siding, on which sat a line of railroad cars. One was a barracks car for the workers, another held the kitchen and mess hall, a third housed the administrative offices and staff quarters, and the fourth was Colonel Deane's private car.

These four cars made up a kind of permanent mobile base camp. Each day, as a new End of Track was reached, a new siding was built and the cars towed to it via steam engine. Cars could be added or subtracted as needed. The colonel's car was first in line, so it could be hitched to an engine and swiftly sped on its way at a moment's notice. The railroad builder had to be ready to respond to any crisis that might break out along the line.

Part of the colonel's car was partitioned off into an office. It was handsomely appointed, with wood paneling, brass fixtures and trim, and carpeting. There was a massive rolltop desk and a couple of glass-fronted bookcases. It was the office of an important personage, a man of affairs, only it was longer and narrower than most. All the heavy furniture was bolted down, ready for travel.

Colonel Deane shooed his associates out, telling them that he didn't want to be interrupted while he was meeting with Slocum. When they were gone, he turned and seized Slocum's hand, vigorously shaking it. "Am I glad to see you!" he said.

"The feeling's mutual, Colonel."

"I owe you more than words can say."

"Then don't say them," Slocum said gruffly.

"Thank God you were there to protect my daughter," Deane said. He was balding, craggy-faced, with an overhanging brow, clear level eyes, a tight straight mouth, and neatly trimmed side-whiskers. He wore a tweed suit and vest, with the pants tucked into the tops of knee-high brown leather engineer's boots. He was a railroader, not a cowboy.

Slocum said, "The gunplay was a tad risky, but not as dangerous as letting outlaws have the upper hand."

"You did right: your work speaks for itself. I shudder to think of Clarissa—or anyone else's daughter!—in the hands of those cutthroats." Deane shook a fist in the air. "The scoundrels! Shooting's too good for them."

"Oh, it was good enough."

"I daresay," Deane said, the father's indignant rage giving way to wryness. He rubbed his temples, blinking, then stared at Slocum.

"I don't know how you do it," he said, wondering. "You've got a knack of popping up unexpectedly at the damnedest times and places—for which I'll be eternally grateful!

"Even before this business, I'd been thinking of getting in touch with you."

"That kind of job, huh?" Slocum asked.

"You're no greenhorn. You were with me when we were building the Denver and Rio Grande line a few years ago, and you remember how rough that got!

"But that was a picnic compared to this job. For out-and-out murderous tactics, this Sovereign line takes the cake!

"I'm no weak sister. Railroading's a tough game, and never tougher than when two different outfits are competing for the same prize. Sabotage, arson, wrecking—you expect all of these in a hard-fought fight.

"This is different. It's deliberate, cold-blooded murder," Deane said. He paced the floor agitated.

"And now they've tried to harm my daughter!" he said.

"To tell the truth, Colonel, and meaning no disrespect, I was surprised that she was going about without any body-guards, things being what they are."

Deane stopped pacing, fixing Slocum with a sharp-eyed

gaze. "No more surprised than I! Do you have any daughters, Slocum?"

"None that I know of."

"If you did, you'd know. Lord knows I do," Deane said. "Clarissa had been visiting some relatives back East, and was due to return home. I'd have been happier if she'd stayed there, but she was afraid of overstaying her welcome. Once she sets her course, it's difficult to dislodge her from it."

"Her father's daughter."

"Ahem. Well. She returned home, escorted by her aunt, Ethel, a most excellent woman, but not used to frontier ways," Deane said. "Apparently they arrived in Denver a few days ago. I say 'apparently' because I knew nothing about it.

"We've had trouble receiving communications here at End of Track. The telegraph lines are down almost daily, and no sooner are they fixed, then they're cut somewhere else along the line. The messages are backed up for days.

"As for couriers, only about half get through, thanks to the holdups and shootings and whatnot. Clarissa couldn't reach me—I had no idea she'd returned.

"So, she decided to come see me at End of Track. With her aunt in tow. A surprise, don't you know?"

"It wasn't a surprise to the gang," Slocum said.

"No, by heaven, it wasn't!"

"Maybe they've got some way of intercepting your messages."

"I'm sure they do," Deane said tartly. "A number of dispatches never reach me—that is, if they're even sent. There's spies everywhere, in the track gangs, the train crews, the telegraphers. . . .

"Of course, we've got our spies in the enemy camp too, so we're not totally stumbling around in the dark," he added, his eyes twinkling for an instant before getting serious again.

"But there's one place we can't get any spies into," the colonel said. "The gang of killers that Sovereign's got working for them.

"Oh, it's all very cleverly done, with nothing to tie them to the gang. That way, they can get their dirty work done, while keeping their hands clean!" Deane colored, his outraged eyes glinting.

"I can fill in the rest," Slocum said. "The bridge was down—"

"Blown up!"

"—so your daughter and the old gal decided to take the barge instead. Up to then, things were pretty much breaking the gang's way."

"And then you came along."

Slocum nodded. "That was luck, pure luck that I was making the crossing at that time. I didn't even know she was your daughter at first. When I found out who she was, I played it like the name didn't mean anything to me. Just out of habit, being cautious."

"To Clarissa's—and my—very good luck!"

Slocum's restless eye fell again and again on a decanter on a sideboard. Deane saw him looking at it.

"That calls for a drink, wouldn't you say?" Deane asked.

"Indeed I would," Slocum said, keeping his gaze fixed on the bottle. He and Deane crossed to the sideboard. The decanter was made of cut crystal, its stopper faceted like a precious jewel. Deane poured the reddish-gold liquid into two fist-sized tumblers.

Slocum said, "The Red Rock line, all the way to Lonesome Canyon."

"Here, here," Deane said. They clinked glasses, drank. The colonel took a sip. Slocum drained his.

''Good stuff,'' Slocum said, rolling the taste around on his tongue.

''Glad you like it,'' Deane said delightedly, refilling Slocum's glass. ''Water?''

''Water I can get anytime,'' Slocum said. He drank some more, slower this time. ''Ah, that's good. It's been a while since I had any of this quality.''

''I'll buy you a case.''

''Done, and thanks.'' And it would be done too.

Deane went behind his desk, but he was too antsy to sit down. Beside the sideboard was an open window. Slocum sat down beside it, enjoying the slight breeze. The air was hazy with dust being kicked up by the work crews. The clangor of their efforts formed a constant backdrop.

Deane paced restlessly out from behind his desk, crossing to the window, looking out. ''It's a simple proposition,'' he said. ''Whoever gets a line to Lonesome Canyon first wins. Loser take nothing. It's hard, but that's the way of it. But this Sovereign bunch fights dirty.''

''You've just got to fight dirtier than them, Colonel.''

''You're the expert.''

''Now that you mention it, I just might be available,'' Slocum said.

''Good man! Now we can start hitting them where it hurts,'' Deane said, smacking a fist into his palm. ''I've got to warn you, though—Sovereign is a very tough outfit.''

''Naturally,'' Slocum said. ''You're going up against Claggard, Truax, and Detheroe.''

The names hung in the air for a few beats. Deane was thoughtful, his lips pursed. ''You're well informed,'' he said.

''About them I am. Too late, but better late than never. When they looted the Emporium Bank in River City, they stole just about all I had. They fixed it up nice and neat, so the law couldn't touch them.

"What they stole from the bank, they used to buy control of the Sovereign Railroad," Slocum said.

"So that's where you come in."

"If Sovereign wins, those three'll make a mountain of money. I'm telling you now, they're not going to win."

"The way you say it, I can hardly doubt you!"

"I'll take their money from them first."

"And then?"

"Slocum rose, smiling thinly. "Much as I'd like to sit around all day drinking your fine whiskey, that ain't going to get the job done."

He looked at his glass, which was empty. "Well, one for the trail couldn't hurt," he said, and had one.

Behind the desk, in a corner, stood a floor safe. It wasn't just bolted down; it was welded in place to the car's frame. Deane went to it, opening the combination lock, swinging open the heavy door. Inside were bonds, notes, piles of greenbacks.

He picked up a bundle of cash and gave it to Slocum. "This'll do for starters," he said.

"More than generous," Slocum said, pocketing the wad.

"You've already earned it. What else do you need? How many men? Name it, and it's yours."

"I work better alone. A lone man can get into more places than a crowd can."

"Well, you know what you're doing," Deane said a little doubtfully. "But for Lord's sake, be careful!"

"Sure. I could use one man, though."

"Who?"

"Crabby—Oliver Crabshaw."

"I know who he is. I know Crabby, that old reprobate."

"He doesn't look like much, and he's kind of a blowhard, but he's a good man in a shooting scrape. I trust him to watch my back. And he knows the country too."

"I think we can spare him," Deane said gravely, hiding a smile.

"Thanks," Slocum said. "There was another man at the barge, a young fellow named Parker."

"Yes, yes, the elusive Mr. Parker! I understand that I have him to thank as well."

Slocum nodded. "He knew what to do and he did it. When he opened up with both barrels of the scattergun on that boat, that pretty much ended it."

"So Clarissa told me. She seemed quite taken with young Parker."

"He's got sand. Might be a good man to have around in a pinch."

"That's what I thought, but I've been unable to meet him. Once my men had arrived at the crossing, he said good-bye to Clarissa and went on his way—to where, I don't know," Deane said.

"Don't be surprised if he turns up again. I have a feeling we haven't seen the last of him."

"If you should run across him in your travels, give him my thanks, and tell him that I'd like to express my appreciation in a more tangible way," Deane said, significantly glancing at the safe so there could be no mistaking his meaning.

"There's a job for him too, if he wants it," Deane added.

"I don't know what he wants, but if I see him, I'll tell him," Slocum said.

He and Deane shook hands again. Slocum crossed to the door, stopped, and turned to face the colonel.

"One more thing," he said. "It might be best to keep it

kind of quiet that I'm working with you, at least for now. "I might have to do some things that the Red Rock might not necessarily want to be associated with."

"I quite understand," Deane said.

13

Near the railroad siding, Crabshaw sat on a tree stump in the shade, using a penknife to whittle away at a stick. At his feet was a small pile of curled wood shavings. A smoking corncob pipe was clenched between his teeth.

Aunt Ethel came striding along, returning from some errand. She climbed the steps to the observation platform at the rear of Deane's car, pausing with her hand on the doorknob when she saw Crabshaw. She led with her chin, pointing with it, looking down her long nose at him.

"Humph! Loafing," she said, outraged.

"Ain't you never heard of lunch?" Crabshaw asked.

"But it's nine o'clock in the morning!"

"So? I ain't eating any lunch, so it's all right." Crabshaw grinned at her stiff back as she went inside the railroad car.

Not long after, Slocum came out, exiting via the front door of the car. The platform at the front was similar to the one at the rear. As Slocum went down the set of steps on the right side, a knot of Deane's underlings climbed those on the left side, crowding into his office, each with something vital for the colonel to decide or sign.

Slocum crossed to Crabshaw. Their horses were tethered nearby, nibbling on green-leafed bushes. Crabshaw rose, folding his penknife and pocketing it. He threw away the sharpened stick he had been working on.

"What's cooking?" he asked.

"Somehow I managed to convince the colonel that he could build the railroad without you," Slocum said. "You're working with me now."

"Hot damn!" In his excitement, Crabshaw blew out of his pipe, sending a mass of orange sparks into the air. When they fell to earth, he did some fancy footwork stamping them out.

"Try not to set the camp on fire," Slocum said dryly. "Think you can stand the pace, old-timer?"

"I'll be raring to go when you've dropped in your tracks, sonny!"

The door opened and Colonel Deane stepped out onto the rear observation platform. He'd escaped his underlings by fleeing through the door into his private quarters, leaving them tangled up with each other in his office. Even a minute's peace and quiet was a luxury.

But he was not to have that minute, for no more than a few seconds after stepping out on the platform, Deane had Aunt Ethel standing at his side, tugging at his elbow.

"Yes, what is it, my dear?" he asked.

With a hissed intake of breath, she indicated Crabshaw, saying, "That man is a lazy good-for-nothing!"

"Who? Mr. Crabshaw?"

"Whatever his name is, that insolent jackanapes."

"On the contrary, he's one of my most trusted men."

She looked sharply at the colonel, as if suspecting him of pulling her leg. But he was straight-faced and seemed serious enough.

"I'm sure I smelled whiskey on his breath—and at nine

o'clock in the morning!'' she said, scandalized.

"It's quite possible," Deane said mildly. "I expect that a railroad camp is more free and easy in some ways that what you're used to back East, Ethel."

"So it seems!"

Slocum and Crabshaw mounted up and rode past the rear of the car. Deane raised a hand in farewell, saying, "Good luck, men."

"Thank'ee, Colonel," Crabshaw said, while Slocum touched a two-fingered salute to his hat brim. When the colonel wasn't looking, Crabshaw screwed up his face and winked at Aunt Ethel.

She gasped, so staggered by his effrontery that she was unable to speak until he'd ridden past. Then, for whatever reason, she decided not to. Her face was pinched and her cheeks were burning.

As they rode side by side, Slocum said, "You're hell with the ladies, Crabby."

"Aw, I was just funning her."

"I think she likes you."

Crabshaw squawked.

"You could do worse," Slocum said. "She's related to the colonel. Marry her, and you could wind up a big man on the railroad."

The other man looked at Slocum as if he had lost his mind. "Marry up with that old battle-ax? Brrr! I'd sooner throw myself under a train," Crabshaw said.

"Well, let's get to work, or you won't have a train to throw yourself under. Or worse, it'll be a Sovereign train," Slocum said.

"Bite your tongue, bub. What's our first move?"

"We're going to do some scouting."

Crabshaw's face fell, disappointed. "Ain't we gonna shoot nobody?"

"All in good time, Mr. Crabshaw, all in good time."

"I better get my gun, just in case."

Slocum raised an eyebrow. "What do you call that hog-leg you're wearing on your hip?"

"That's just a side gun. I'm talking about a big gun. You'll see," Crabshaw said. They were on the ground between the siding and the main line, pointing northward. Crabshaw turned his horse toward a middle car on the supply train, an equipment car. He stepped out of the saddle, swinging himself up on to the rear platform, where he tied the horse's reins to a rail, and went into the car.

A few minutes later he returned, lugging over one shoulder a rifle that was longer than he was. "Big fifty," he said. "Buffalo gun, fifty-caliber."

"That'll blow a big enough hole in the landscape," Slocum said. "Too bad there's no buffalo."

"Waal," Crabshaw drawled, "I reckon I'll find something to shoot."

"Could be."

Crabshaw rigged the long rifle so that it hung slanted on the side of the saddle, out of the way. He mounted up, but before they could go, along came Clarissa Deane.

She was in Western attire, wearing a hat, a short jacket, a long skirt, and boots. Trailing a respectful few paces behind her were two men, one young and handsome, the other jowly and grizzled. They both wore side guns and looked as if they could use them.

Clarissa halted, the others stopping too. They moved so they were flanking her. They did it nicely, without making a fuss about it, but it definitely was a protective posture. The two men's faces were closed, wary.

"Howdy, Miss Clarissa. Howdy, Al, Jeff," Crabshaw said, nodding first to the older man, then to the younger.

Indicating his companion, he said, "He's okay, boys. This here's Slocum."

Al and Jeff exchanged glances. It was clear that they recognized the name. They eased up slightly, knowing that the stranger was on their side.

"Good morning, Mr. Crabshaw. Mr. Slocum," Clarissa said.

"Miss Deane," Slocum said, politely touching his hat brim.

"I was hoping I'd see you again so I could thank you properly for what you did yesterday. And to apologize for letting those men get away. Did you ever catch them?"

"No, ma'am," he said, remembering how he had last seen Len, Reese, and Curly, sprawled dead in the cold, moonlit clearing off the trail. "But I doubt that they'll be bothering us again," he said.

"Today I realize that I acted like a fool, but at the time, I suppose I became a bit fainthearted. I just wanted the killing to stop."

"Don't worry about it. I'm sure it all turned out for the best."

"I hope so," she said, biting her lower lip. Then she brightened. "I'd also like to thank Mr. Parker too. Have you seen him?"

"Sorry, no."

"Oh. Oh, that's too bad. I was hoping . . . well, never mind."

"If I do see him, I'll be sure to let him know."

"Would you? That would be splendid! My father would like to talk to him about a job working for the railroad."

"If I see him, I'll tell him, miss."

"Thank you, Mr. Slocum."

"You're welcome, ma'am. See you." Slocum touched

his hat again, then nodded to Al and Jeff. He and Crabshaw went on their way.

When they had gone a short distance, Crabshaw said, "The colonel's got Jeff Coles looking after Clarissa, guarding her."

"Which one was he?"

"The good-looking feller. He's good with a gun too."

"And the other one?"

"That's Al Markand. He's guarding Jeff! You know, in case he gets any ideas about romancing the boss's daughter."

"I'd say she's got ideas of her own, about Parker."

"Mebbe so. What do you know about him, Slocum?"

"What? I thought you knew just about everybody this side of the Mississippi, Crabby."

"I ain't seen this Parker fellow yet. What's he like?"

Slocum thought about it for a minute. "He doesn't hesitate when it comes time to pull the trigger."

"That's good, ain't it?" Crabshaw asked.

"Depends on what side he's on."

"What side is he on?"

"We'll find out."

"You got to find him first."

"Later. First, we'll go look at the battlefield," Slocum said.

14

The land fronting the pass was relatively flat plains, divided by the road from town. The Red Rock line had outriders patrolling beyond the railhead, and so did Sovereign. The two were still far enough away so that the riders were out of shooting distance of each other. The center strip was a corridor connecting the mine with the town. There wasn't much traffic on it, mostly supply wagons going back and forth, and they didn't linger while making their runs.

Slocum had Crabshaw take him around to meet the riders on patrol. "That way they won't shoot me when I'm poking around," he explained. He kept in the background, letting Crabshaw do most of the talking, getting across the idea that he had approval from on high to do whatever he was doing, and whatever it was, it would be best for them to ignore it. They got the idea. They weren't railroaders; they were gunmen, professionals.

"Nice hard-bitten bunch," Slocum said as he and Crabshaw rode on after making their rounds of the outriders.

"That's what's needed," Crabshaw said. "Sovereign's got more of the same, and worse."

"I know, I've seen the worse." Slocum told him of his night ride into Black Diamond country.

"Thunderation!" Crabshaw exclaimed after hearing the tale. "What'd the colonel say when you told him that?"

"I didn't tell him."

"Huh? Why in the Sam Hill not?"

"The colonel's still hot about them making a try for his daughter. First thing he'd do is try to clean up the gang."

"Sounds like a pretty good idea to me!"

"You wouldn't think so when the gang started using you for target practice. And that's just what it would be, target practice—for them," Slocum said. "Nobody's knocking Gussie out of that canyon by coming straight on at him. A couple of guns could hold it against an army. A frontal attack would be suicide."

"Makes sense," Crabshaw conceded reluctantly. "But it sticks in my craw to let 'em get away with it!"

"They're not getting away with it. They'll be called to account, to pay in full."

Crabshaw was skeptical. "That's tall talk, pard'ner, but how do you plan to make it come about? Especially since you ain't minded to go charging in after those rascals."

"We don't go to them, we make them come to us," Slocum said. "And we won't have to do much. Gus won't set up in that canyon, waiting for things to happen. He's going to want to make them happen, and to do that, he's got to come down out of the hills.

"The tracklaying contest is in its last laps. You can be sure that Gus'll strike soon. He has to, if he wants to affect the outcome. It won't do Sovereign any good for him to act once the race is won, one way or the other.

"But Gussie'll do whatever's best for him, even if it's not what's best for his employers. Having him siding you can be as bad as having him against you."

They rode east, away from the pass. After they had gone a few paces, Crabshaw said, "You know Gus Andrews pretty good?"

"I know him," Slocum said. "He's a real bad son of Texas. He's a cowboy, started out as a drover on some of those big cattle drives up to Kansas. Came up at the same time as Wes Hardin, King Fisher, that crowd. Most of them are dead or in jail, but not Gus. He was ramrod for Shanghai Pierce, the blowhard cattle baron. Whenever ol' Shanghai's outfit was tearing up a town, Gus was doing most of the tearing. When Gus and his circle quit to go off on their own, that pretty much took all the steam out of Pierce.

"Gus turned outlaw and he's been going strong ever since."

"Maybe we can fix that, huh?" Crabshaw asked.

"We'd better, or he'll fix us."

Slocum pointed his horse south and Crabshaw followed, asking, "Where we going now?"

"We'll follow the line a ways," Slocum said.

Crabshaw gestured with his thumb, indicating the pass. "That's where the fighting's gonna be."

"You think so, huh?"

"There's one best right-of-way through to Lonesome Canyon, and both sides want it. When it looks like one or t'other is going to get there first, things'll start popping, mark my words!"

Crabshaw had reined in his horse while talking, but Slocum had continued on ahead, forcing Crabshaw to spur his horse to catch up to him.

"Ain't you heard a thing I said?" Crabshaw demanded.

"I heard."

"Then you ain't listening. What for are you going that-away?"

"Gussie hasn't stayed alive this long by doing the expected. Everybody knows there's going to be a fight at the pass, right? You can count on Gus to come at you from the opposite direction,'' Slocum said.

"I get you, bub. Kind of a contrary fellow, eh?''

"He's a rustler and a raider. That's how he started and that's how he'll finish. Hit hard, using speed and surprise. I know how he thinks.''

"You know, because you're one yourself.''

"As if you haven't thrown a rope over a few choice brands belonging to somebody else!''

"I done worse than that,'' Crabshaw said eagerly, launching into a boastful account of some of his misadventures.

It was a good day for riding. The sun was warm, the air was crisp, and the horses stepped lively. They rode parallel to the tracks, a few hundred yards east of them. West of the line were the cliffs.

The line kept well clear of the falling-rock zone, but a few miles south of the pass, a spur of the cliff thrust well out onto the flat. Not far from it was an arroyo. Here, because of the narrow strip of land, the line hugged the curve of the bulging rock limb.

The two riders halted at the foot of the spur, insects at the foot of a giant's castle. Rock walls rose up and up, thrusting skyward for hundreds of feet. Near the top the walls bulged outward, creating a massive overhang.

Slocum looked up, head bent back. "How do you get to the top?''

"You don't, 'lessen you're some kind of fly that can walk up walls,'' Crabshaw said.

"There's no way up there?''

"There's a trail to the top, but it's way to hell and gone on the other side of the rocks, in the pass.''

"That's the only way up?''

"See any others?"

"No."

"Well, that's the only way up," Crabshaw said.

"Can you ride on it?" Slocum asked.

"You could, I suppose, but why would you want to? Ain't nothing up there."

Slocum was interested in the site. He got off his horse and walked around, circling back and forth under the spur, crossing to the edge of the arroyo and looking down into it, scanning the knobby cliff top from various angles.

South of the spur, the cliffs once more gave ground to the flatland, widening the strip between them and the arroyo. The right-of-way swung out from under the shadow of the rocks, while the arroyo dwindled to a cut in the earth, then a ditch, merging insensibly with the sprawling plains.

Not far beyond, the line began its long sweeping eastward curve toward the river.

Again Slocum eyed the spur. "That's where I'd do it."

"Do what?" Crabshaw asked.

"I've seen enough. Let's head back," Slocum said. He pointed his horse north and rode, Crabshaw following.

15

They had just started away from the tracks when they saw three riders coming from the south. The newcomers weren't coming at a run, but they weren't walking either.

Slocum and Crabshaw halted up. "Are they our boys or theirs?" Slocum asked.

"Well, now, I can't rightly tell. They're too far away," Crabshaw said. "No, wait a minute, I can see 'em now. They're our boys."

Slocum took his hand away from his gun, but not too far away. "So we don't get to shoot anyone yet."

"Or get shot at," Crabshaw said. He and Slocum pointed their horses at the newcomers, and waited. The others slowed as they neared, halting when within hailing distance. They were Red Rock gunmen, different from the ones Slocum had met before, and yet somehow the same. They knew Crabshaw and greeted him familiarly.

"This here's Slocum," Crabshaw said. "He's okay."

The middle rider, the leader of the group, said, "We saw you on the tracks, didn't know you at first, so we came for a look-see. Thought you might be wreckers. Ain't likely that them varmints would make a move in broad daylight, but—who knows?''

"You patrolling the tracks?" Slocum asked.

The rider looked questioningly at Crabshaw. "He's okay, I tell ya," Crabshaw said. "He's the man that gunned down them jaspers at the crossing."

The riders broke into smiles. "That was nice work," said the one on the left. The leader said, "Glad to know you, mister," and the third man nodded.

They answered Slocum's questions readily enough. It turned out that they were the counterpart of the armed men who were patrolling the no-man's-land between the two oncoming rail lines. "We've been running patrols up and down the right-of-way, night and day, ever since they blew up the bridge," the leader explained. "There's other patrols out here with us, staggered up and down along the line so no part of it is ever out of sight for too long."

"Seen anything suspicious?" Slocum asked.

"Just you," the other said, grinning. The grin vanished quick enough as he added, "We know that Sovereign's going to make another try, though. It's just a matter of where and when."

"When is liable to be pretty soon."

"Reckon so."

"Where? That's the question," Slocum said. That broke up the parley, as the two groups went their separate ways, Slocum and Crabshaw riding north.

"Where to now?" Crabshaw asked.

"I want to climb that cliff top—"

"What in tarnation for?"

"—but it's getting a little long in the day for that now," Slocum said. "I want to look around up there when it's light. We'll head up there tomorrow, leave before dawn.

For now, though, let's keep heading north. I want to see the Sovereign line.''

Crabshaw looked at him a little dubiously. ''If you want to go poking around, let's wait till after dark. Sovereign's got patrols same as we do, only they're not liable to be too sociable if they catch us around the tracks. Unless it's fireworks you're after?''

''Not yet,'' Slocum said. ''We'll stick a safe distance away. But I want to scout out the lay of the land while there's still daylight.''

The sun was about midway in the western sky, its lower rim only a few degrees of arc from grazing the mountain peaks. Blue shadows began creeping eastward from the base of the range, spreading like a lake in flood.

The two riders crossed the road to town and continued northward, following a course about an eighth of a mile east of, and parallel to, the line of cliffs above the mouth of the pass.

The scene was a mirror image of that taking place in the south, as the Sovereign Railroad thrust toward its goal. There was that same wedge-shaped vanguard at the head of the line, a multi-limbed beast made up of hundreds of work crew members clearing and grading and tracklaying, From a distance, the opposing lines looked like twin columns of warring giant ant colonies, closing in for battle. At the railheads, where the work pace was at its most furious, twin dust clouds climbed into the sky, standing out in the sunlight that backlit them.

Slocum and Crabshaw left the scene of activity behind as they continued north. After a mile or so, the right-of-way entered a lonely flat, and stretched across it, arcing northeast in a wide curve a few miles further on.

There were Sovereign riders patrolling the line, but Slocum and Crabshaw steered clear of it and them. ''Of course, if they want to come over and make trouble, that's another story,'' Slocum said.

''Don't bother them, and they won't bother you,'' Crabshaw said. ''They're too smart to break the law out in the open.''

''I thought the marshal doesn't lift a finger outside town.''

''He don't. But if either side pulls something too raw, the governor'll have to step in, declare martial law, and send in the troops. That's why Sovereign's got the Black Diamond bunch. They can rob and wreck and kill, and the line can say, 'Don't blame us, it's outlaws that're making the trouble.' ''

The landscape was similar to that south of the pass, but there was no spur of rock outthrusting from the cliffs to edge the tracks before they made the great swerve away to the northeast.

Blue-purple shadows lapped the tracks, rolling eastward. The sun dropped behind the rocks, causing an instant ten-degree temperature drop. Cool winds blew down from the hills.

Slocum and Crabshaw halted, facing the far-off northeastern line. They turned their horses and headed south. Shadows were purple now. The crews continued to work. They would keep on working as long as there was light to see by.

When the two men reached the pass, they could see a few pinpoints of light winking in the town. Nearer, the two railroads had narrowed the gap between them by a few miles less than the day before.

''We're beating 'em,'' Crabshaw said, judiciously eyeing the relative positions of the dual railheads. ''We've had the lead on 'em in mileage for the last couple of days,'' he said.

"The race is not always to the swift," Slocum said.

Crabshaw looked at him. "That's in the Bible, ain't it?"

"I don't know. I heard it from a gambler who used to fix horse races."

"That's dirty business."

"Not if you bet the winner."

Crabshaw pointed his horse toward the Red Rock railhead. "Where are you going?" Slocum asked.

"Why, back to camp naturally."

"Uh-uh. Let's go to town instead."

"But it's almost supper time!" Crabshaw protested.

"We'll eat in town," said Slocum.

"I can guess where—at that redheaded widow's cafe."

"It's good food."

"Maybe, but that ain't what you got a hankering for."

"Never mind about that," Slocum said. "A man's got to eat dinner somewhere."

"There's a perfectly good mess hall back at the camp!" Crabshaw sniffed the air. "Why, I can smell that food a-cooking on the campfire."

"Smells like hot tar."

"We're almost there, and town's a long ways away. I can hear my stomach rumbling, I'm so starved."

"Hey, I'm still working, pardner. I've got business in town."

"Well, why didn't you say so in the first place? That's different."

They turned their horses toward town and started east along the road. "Still, a man's got to eat," Slocum said. "We'll have us a first-class feed on the colonel's money."

"Now you're talking, bub."

"And drink," Slocum added.

"Hot damn!"

"And then we'll make trouble."

16

It was dusk when they reached town. The jailhouse fronted on the courthouse square, a fifty-year-old one-story thick-walled stone blockhouse. Its long side faced the square. A roofed-over wooden porch edged the front of the building. A few empty wooden chairs stood against the stone wall. The windows were few, high and narrow, like slits. Light shone through them onto the ground in front of the building.

Slocum and Crabshaw reined in at the jail. Crabshaw said, "What about that big feed you was talking about?"

"Business first," Slocum said.

"What business you got with the marshal anyhow?"

"Lawman business." Slocum and Crabshaw stepped down from their mounts and tied them to a hitching post.

"I'll wait out here, if you don't mind," Crabshaw said. "I don't want to get no closer to the inside of a jail than I have to."

The front door opened and two men came out, big men with shotguns and badges—deputies. They were about to make their rounds. When they saw Slocum, their tough blunt faces got harder and more skeptical. He nodded politely as he brushed past them to go inside. They stood facing the door through which he'd passed.

A half minute passed with no ruckus from inside, so they shrugged and turned away, seeing Crabshaw standing near the horses at the hitching post.

"What do you want?" one of the deputies asked.

"I'm waiting for him," Crabshaw said, meaning Slocum.

"What does he want?" the other one asked.

"Derned if I know!" The way he said it, they knew he meant it, but that didn't mean they liked it. They looked at each other, then continued on their way, angling across the square.

Inside, half the jailhouse was taken up by the marshal's office, while the other half held the cells. The marshal sat behind a wooden desk, facing the doors. To one side, a deputy stood beside a potbellied stove, pouring himself a cup of coffee from a pot that had been warming on the flat lid of the stove.

Beyond lay the cells, a quartet of black wrought-iron cages paired two by two, facing each other across a central aisle. The cages held a couple of glum, dispirited prisoners.

The marshal looked like a banker, except for his badge and gun. The deputy looked like a deputy, beetle-browed, burly, and suspicious of the newcomer.

Slocum went to the desk and stood facing the seated man. The marshal looked up at him, his eyes bright, interested, the rest of his face stony blank.

"The name's Slocum, Marshal. I'd like to talk a little business with you."

The lawman moved his chair closer to the desk, while his expression remained the same: bright-eyed, blank-faced.

"You buying or selling?" the lawman asked.

"Nope," Slocum said. "Cashing in."

The deputy stood holding the coffeepot in one hand and a cup in the other, watching the back-and-forth between Slocum and the marshal. Little spirals of steam came ribboning out of the coffee spout.

The marshal rested his elbows on the desk, hands pressed together, forming a steeple. He nodded for Slocum to go on.

"Some outlaws were killed at the crossing yesterday," Slocum said. "I killed them."

"Good for you."

"I figured there might be some bounties on them."

"And you figured you'd collect them, eh? Can you prove it?"

"A half-dozen or so witnesses'll swear to it."

The marshal smiled without parting his lips. It didn't last long, but then it wasn't much of a smile. "Hear that, Kinsley?"

"Sure did, Mitt," the deputy said, grinning. Mitt looked from him to Slocum. "One problem, mister," he said.

"What's that, Marshal?" Slocum asked.

"Another fellow came in this morning and laid the same claim. Young fellow, a tall galoot name of Parker." The marshal laid his hands down palms-flat on the desktop. "Now what've you got to say about that?" he asked.

"It's a fair claim," Slocum said.

"Is that right?"

"Parker got some of them and so did I. There's two that I got for sure, though."

"Which ones?"

"The preacher, and some hombre named Pete Polk."

Kinsley grunted, then laughed. "The two big-money ones."

The marshal nodded. "More power to you if you did get them, stranger—"

"I did. Or did Parker say different?"

"Fact is, he didn't say much, he just asked about putting in a claim on any reward."

"Is there a reward, Marshal?"

"On some of them. On the ones you say you killed. I'll tell you what I told Parker. After we hold the inquest, if your claim holds up, you can put in for your money."

"When's the inquest?"

The marshal shrugged. "Tomorrow maybe. Or the day after."

"Parker in town?" Slocum asked.

The marshal smiled again, this time showing his teeth. He held the smile for a moment. "Figuring on looking him up, having a little talk with him about the blood money? And then there was one. Or maybe none, if you kill each other off."

"Then you won't have to pay the money," Slocum said.

"Parker was in town this morning. Could be he's still around. I've got a hunch he won't go too far until the matter of the reward money's settled. We'll want him to testify at the inquest. You too."

"I'll be around. I've got a payday coming."

"We'll see," the marshal said.

Slocum turned to go. Kinsley poured himself a cup of coffee and put the pot down on top of the stove.

"Pete Polk's got some friends hereabouts," Kinsley said, not unfriendly.

"That so? Any of them got prices on their heads?" Slocum asked.

"All of them."

The marshal said, "Go up to Black Diamond canyon and shoot anyone you see, and chances are they'll have a price tag on them. And the town'll be happy to pay it."

"I'll keep it in mind."

"Good. And here's something else for you to keep in mind." The marshal was serious now, the facestiousness over.

"You bounty killers can do as you like outside of town. You can kill each other, for all I care. It'll help simplify the bookkeeping. But whatever you do, make sure you do it outside the city limits. Anybody that shoots up my town, for whatever reason, gets cracked down on hard, savvy?"

Slocum nodded. "Fair enough. But when somebody attacks me, I defend myself—no matter where I am. Savvy?"

"Then don't get attacked in town," the marshal said, coming right back at him.

"That hold for Boom Town too?"

"Hell, no! You can burn down the whole miserable pesthole, for all I care. Those bastards down there don't pay my salary. Just don't bring your troubles north of the deadline, that's all. Down there you can do what you want."

Slocum went to the door. "See you."

"Be here for the inquest," the marshal called after him.

17

The Mountainview Hotel fronted the square, diagonally opposite the jailhouse. It was the best hotel in town, a two-story structure with peaked roofs, gables, dormers, and turrets at the front corners. It was a white wooden gingerbread castle. There was a big front stairway and a roofed-over veranda encircling three sides of the building.

Slocum and Crabshaw rode past it. The hotel was ablaze with light. Through broad glass panes could be seen glimpses of the lobby: the back of an armchair, a potted plant, a glittering chandelier, and the distant curve of a grand staircase. Small knots of well-dressed men and women were grouped on the veranda and inside.

"Getting a look at how the other half lives? Or have you got business here too?" Crabshaw asked.

"Just looking," Slocum said. "This is the kind of place that certain parties I'm interested in would stay at."

"How do you know they ain't here now?"

"No guards. When they come, they'll have their *pistoleros* out, keeping an eye out for the likes of you and me."

"Especially you, huh? Heh-heh. When that day comes, I want to see it!"

"Maybe you will."

"Not if I die of hunger first! Thought you said something about getting some chow," Crabshaw said accusingly. "What're we hanging around here for? Ain't nothing to be seen but a bunch of duded-up highbinders, tinhorns, bottom-dealers, and their fancy women."

"You answered your own question. Some of those fancy women are pretty fancy," Slocum said.

A man and woman crossed the veranda, coming out of the shadows into the light. They were strangers to Slocum, not that he wouldn't have minded getting to know the woman better. Her shapely form, outlined against the light, belonged to one worth knowing.

A figure bobbed into view on the ground below the veranda, in the bushes. A man, who rose up as the couple stepped into the light. They didn't see him, had no idea he was there.

The lurker crouched, staring intently at the male half of the couple as the duo went under the light. For an instant, the man's profile was clearly revealed, his features as sharp as if etched on a coin.

Whoever the lurker sought, this was not the man. The lurker bared his teeth and made a fist and shook it.

Oblivious, the couple went inside. Another man came out of the hotel, a well-fed guest who stepped to one side and lit a cigar. He too came all unknowing under the scrutiny of the lurker in the bushes, who peered up at him through the vertical bars of the porch railing. The smoker got his cigar going and puffed away, tossing an extinguished match off the porch, inadvertently almost hitting the lurker. The smoker strolled away, haloed by a cloud of smoke.

Slocum and Crabshaw were watching the lurker. "Reckon he's tetched?" Crabshaw asked out of the side of his mouth.

"Could be," Slocum said. "The last time I saw him, he was in a hotel room in River City, trying to work up the nerve to kill himself."

The lurker was Austin Pritchard, the fugitive former clerk of the Emporium Bank, who'd been left holding the bag for its absconded assets by Claggard, Truax, and Detheroe.

"You know him?" Crabshaw asked, low-voiced.

"I know all the crackbrains," Slocum said, glancing significantly at Crabshaw.

"That's because you drove 'em all loco."

"Not this one."

"He seems to be doing a pretty good job of it by himself," Crabshaw observed dryly.

Pritchard looked like a caricature of a desperate character, wild-haired, wild-eyed, skulking around in the bushes. Suddenly he started, ducking out of sight. Rustling among the bushes showed he was making his way behind their cover to the corner of the building.

"Wonder what spooked him?" Crabshaw asked. He and Slocum glanced in the direction Pritchard had been looking before he had left.

They saw two deputies approaching, the same ones who'd set out earlier from the jailhouse. The two walked side by side, shotguns tucked under their arms pointing downward, pacing shoulder to shoulder. Between the two of them, they took up most of the wooden plank sidewalk bordering the square. Those who were in their way stepped aside, even if they had to duck into a doorway or step down into the street to do it.

The deputies walked unconcernedly, making their routine rounds. They hadn't seen Pritchard, who'd taken off upon seeing them. They did see Slocum and Crabshaw, betraying it by a slight stiffening of their pace.

"Howdy," Crabshaw said, nodding to them. Slocum touched two fingers to his hat brim. The deputies came on, not altering their mechanical stride, the two of them stepping off together like clockwork.

"No loitering," one said.

"Move along," said the other.

Slocum and Crabshaw urged their horses onward and away. "Who was that galoot in the bushes?" Crabshaw asked.

"I'll tell you later," Slocum said.

"Tell me over some grub. I'm starving!"

Crabshaw pushed his chair away from the table and patted his bulging belly with both hands. "I'm stuffed! If I et another piece of pie, I'd bust!"

"That's okay, you already ate the last piece," Slocum said. "Plus a mess of just about everything else on the menu."

"And right good it was too, son. Now I'm ready for some drinking."

"You don't say," Slocum said sarcastically. They were in the cafe, where they sat leaning back from the table after a big meal. It was a corner table, and they sat facing the door. The main dining hour had passed, but there were a half-dozen other patrons scattered around the tables. The space was warm, filled with yellow-gold light and good food smells.

Slocum pushed back his chair, rising. Crabshaw looked worried, saying, "Hey, where you going?"

"Don't get yourself in an uproar, Crabby. I'm just going to pay my compliments to the owner," Slocum said.

"That's a relief. I thought you were leaving so I'd have to pay for the grub."

"You couldn't pay it, with all you ate. They'd have you in the back washing dishes."

"Watch out that redheaded woman don't have *you* washing dishes," Crabshaw said, grinning.

Across the room, Eileen Barrett stood behind a waist-high wooden counter, ostentatiously doing her accounts in a leather-bound ledger.

Slocum went to her. She looked up, her face motionless, masklike, except for the eyes. They were bright, vivid, mocking. "You must like my cooking, cowboy," she said.

"I surely do, and that's a fact, ma'am," Slocum said.

"See anything else around here you like? Maybe you're interested in the specialty of the house."

"What's that?"

"Your heart's desire," she said seriously.

"What's *your* heart's desire?" he asked.

"If you're really interested, you've already asked around and you know."

"Nothing like hearing it from the horse's mouth—er, well, you know."

"A dead man is my heart's desire," she said. "Silverado. Bring me Silverado dead, and you can have your heart's desire. Otherwise, don't bother to come around."

She closed the ledger, tucking it under her arm. She came out from behind the counter and went down the passage past the kitchen, turning a corner and out of sight.

Slocum stood there, thoughtful. The conversation had been held in low tones, with no one nearby to overhear them. It was strange to talk of trading blood for flesh in the homey surroundings of a cafe, the setting making the words seem even more unreal.

He waited, but she did not return. Shrugging, he went back to his table and sat down. "Looks like you didn't do so good," Crabshaw said. "There's only one way to thaw that snow maiden, and that's to bring her Silverado's head.''

"I'm going to have to do something about that boy," Slocum said. "He's seriously interfering with my love life."

The waitress came around with more coffee. It was the same blank-faced young serving girl from the day before. This time, she was smirking.

"She ain't gonna come out till you're gone, so if you're hanging around waiting for her, you're wasting your time," she said.

"I'm glad you told me that before I left the tip," Slocum said.

Her face fell, the smirk turning down at the corners. "Don't blame me! She told me to tell you that, mister!"

"That's okay, I wasn't going to tip you anyway. Just funning," he added quickly. "Just having a little fun with you, that's all."

He settled the bill, adding a generous tip that put the smirk back on her lips. True to her word, the redhead never reappeared.

Slocum and Crabshaw went out into the bracing night air. "You gave that shifty-faced brat too much money," Crabshaw said.

"I'm going to eat there again, and I don't want her spitting into my food," Slocum said.

"She'll probably do it anyhow. Struck me as the spiteful type."

They moved away from the revealing light pouring out the cafe front, moving down the street, where it was darker.

"That was a mighty good feed, pard'ner. Thank'ee," Crabshaw said.

"Don't mention it," Slocum said.

Crabshaw reached into a belt-pouch and pulled out two

cigars, offering one to Slocum. "Smoke?" he asked.

Slocum took the cigar. It was fresh, aromatic. It was a good cigar, a damned good cigar. He rolled it under his nose, inhaling.

"Wait a minute," he said, "this is one of Colonel Deane's cigars."

"He gave 'em to me! What do you think I did, stole 'em?!"

"Nooooo . . ."

"You're so damned fussy, give it back then!" Crabshaw grabbed for the cigar, but Slocum was quicker, snatching it away from his grasp.

"It's a good cigar," Slocum said when he had it lit and was puffing away on it.

"Huh! Ain't so partickaler now, are you, bub?" Crabshaw sneered, also surrounded by clouds of cigar smoke.

They smoked their cigars and went to where the horses were hitched. "Might be a long night," Crabshaw said. "Reckon we ought to board our animals at the livery stable?"

"We're going to want to have our horses saddled and ready to ride at all times," Slocum said.

"It's going to be that kind of a night, huh? Hot damn!" Crabshaw rubbed his palms together. "Where do we start?"

"I was figuring on a little kidnapping first," Slocum said.

18

Slocum saved half the cigar and smoked it on the veranda of the Mountainview Hotel. He didn't look out of place at the fancy hotel. In the rough-and-ready frontier society of the West, a cattle baron might dress like a cowhand, and not be judged on anything apart from the size of his money roll. That was real democracy at work. Besides, Slocum carried himself so that no matter where he was, he looked like he belonged.

From inside the lobby came the rise and fall of conversation, the buzz of many voices. It was a lively scene, one of the few in the town proper north of the deadline. A good part of the town was already locked up and dark for the night, but not here. Here was where all the businessmen stayed, the financiers, mining and railroad stock promoters, would-be concessionaires, salesmen seeking commissions, and other vendors, all looking to cash in on the bonanza that would result once a railroad linked up with the Lonesome Canyon mines. With the big men were their assistants, clerks, bookkeepers, and the like.

Mixed in with the rest were the confidence men, swindlers, phony stock promoters, and all the rest of the magpie breed who feathered their own nests at the expense of the less astute. The only way to tell them apart from their legitimate business counterparts was that the rogues generally looked more upright and self-importantly respectable.

And then there were the women. The junction wasn't a place for wives and sweethearts; it was mistresses and whores. Some of the money men brought their kept women along, but there was a large pool of whores circulating through the hotel. The smell of money had attracted some of the freshest and best-looking young whores in the territory. They had to have a certain ladylike decorum in the hotel, and those who didn't were politely but firmly escorted out of the lobby, with instructions not to return. Those who did, or persisted in being troublesome, were turned over to the deputies for their amusement, and then hustled across the line into Boom Town. In Boom Town they could do as they liked, sink or swim, nobody gave a damn.

The lobby bar did a brisk business, and the clinking of bottles and glasses sounded over the waves of conversation. Inside, it was a whirl of color, light, motion.

Slocum had his back turned to it as he stood at a front corner of the porch, leaning against the railing, smoking a cigar. He peered down into the bushes, seeing only bushes.

Two deputies marched past in lockstep, making their rounds, the same two he'd seen earlier. They barely glanced at the hotel front as they passed, and certainly didn't see Slocum. He blew smoke rings at their backs.

The porch was raised about four feet above the ground. There was a sense of rustling motion among the shadowed bushes. . . .

A figure crouched low, bent almost double, apelike, creeping between the bushes and the porch.

Slocum looked around. The veranda was more or less

deserted. Earlier, there had been a number of people taking the air, but since then it had gotten chilly and most of them had gone inside. A few men stood to one side of the front entrance, smoking and chatting. One of them casually glanced Slocum's way, but that was all.

Things were happening below. Light shining through a broad high window thrust a long yellow rectangle across the porch and the ground beyond. The figure huddled outside the light, but close enough to the edge that his face could be seen.

It was Pritchard, wild-eyed, gnashing his teeth. And that was before he knew he'd been seen by somebody on the porch. Slocum leaned over the rail and said, "Psst! Pritchard!" He pitched his voice low, so it wouldn't carry.

The effect on Pritchard was electrifying. He went rigid, as if paralyzed by a stroke. All except for his neck muscles, which tilted his head backward as he looked up to see who had called his name.

He saw Slocum. He reeled, clapping a hand to his jacket pocket. Before he could reach inside, there was a loud *clonk!*

It was the sound of Crabshaw laying the barrel of his gun across the back of Pritchard's head. Crabshaw had risen from where he'd been crouching behind the unsuspecting Pritchard, clubbing him smartly.

Pritchard dropped, unconscious. Crabshaw looked around, holstering his gun. He crouched over Pritchard, dragging him deeper into the shadows.

"Nice work," Slocum said, nodding.

"Sneaking up on somebody is child's play for an old mountain man like me," Crabshaw said.

"It is easy," a voice said, speaking conversationally, in contrast to Slocum and Crabshaw's stage whispers. The speaker stood behind Slocum, who was surprised and a little bit irked that somebody could sneak up on him without his knowing it.

It was Parker, jaunty derby hat and all. He was affable, easy. "You again," Slocum said.

"I'm staying at the hotel," Parker said.

"You're coming up in the world."

Parker shrugged, moving past Slocum to the rail. He nodded at Crabshaw, who stood frozen on the ground, looking up. "I don't know you," Parker said. Then to Slocum. "Hope I'm not interrupting anything."

"We're helping out a friend," Slocum said. He significantly touched the side of his head a few times. "The poor fellow's sick in the head. Harmless, but he has fits."

"Too bad."

"We're trying to handle it without a fuss—for the sake of the family, you understand."

Parker nodded. "I'll give you a hand."

"Thanks, but we can handle it by ourselves."

"I insist."

Slocum looked at him. "What's your game, Parker?"

"What's yours? I'm thinking that we didn't do too badly the last time we teamed up. It'd be a shame to have talent like that working at cross-purposes."

"That's a point."

"Well . . . what now?"

Crabshaw spoke from below. "How about giving me a hand with this consarned idjit?"

"Who's that?" Parker asked, frowning.

"That's Crabby. Don't worry about him, he's harmless," Slocum said.

Crabshaw squawked, outraged.

"Not him," Parker said quickly, "the other one. I saw him sneaking around the hotel earlier today. He loco or something?"

"Yes and no," Slocum said. "It's a long story. But he

could be useful.'' He went down some wooden steps to the ground, Parker following.

Pritchard's feet and legs up to the knees stuck out past the bushes, stretching onto the lawn. Holes were worn through the soles of his shoes, and his threadbare clothing was soiled and frayed. Even unconscious, his pale lumpy face was taut, anxious.

''Your cub's grown a few fangs,'' Crabshaw said, holding up a gun. ''I found this in his pocket.''

''Hang on to it,'' Slocum said.

''No, I was gonna give it back to him as soon as he woke up,'' Crabshaw said sarcastically.

''We've got to get him out of here,'' Slocum said.

''Here's an idea,'' Parker said. ''Instead of getting him out of here, why don't we get him into here?''

''Why not?'' said Slocum.

So it was that, not long afterwards, Slocum and Crabshaw each took an arm of the semi-conscious Pritchard and hauled him up and out from behind the bushes and onto his feet. They stood on either side of him, supporting him.

Parker stood on the porch stairs, gesturing for them to come on. Slocum and Crabshaw half-walked, half-dragged Pritchard up the stairs. He was starting to come around, rolling his head and moaning.

Slocum and Crabshaw walked him across the veranda, following Parker a few paces ahead. Pritchard came around and started struggling. Crabshaw *clonked* him on the back of the head again with the gun barrel. Pritchard went limp, head and knees sagging. Slocum and Crabshaw each had one of his arms across their shoulders. Crabshaw took off his own hat and pulled it down on Pritchard's head, so it covered his face.

Parker motioned for the others to wait. He went inside, returning a minute later with three young women in tow, a blonde and two brunettes, all good-looking and shapely. They'd each had a few drinks and were in high spirits.

The blonde asked Parker, "Who're your friends, honey?"

One of the two brunettes said, "Looks like a party."

The other brunette eyed Pritchard, sagging in the other's arms, and said, "Looks like he's had a little too much party!"

"The rest of us'll just have to make up for it," Parker said. "We'll take this poor fellow up to the room to sleep it off first."

The group went inside, into the lobby. The walls echoed with loud talk and laughter. Slocum and Crabshaw waltzed Pritchard past the front desk. "Can't hold his liquor," Parker said, breezing past the night clerk. The night clerk nodded, not giving a damn so long as he didn't have to lift a finger to help.

Slocum and Crabshaw had their work cut out for them in carrying Pritchard up the main staircase to the second floor. It got easier when Parker came up behind them and hooked a hand inside Pritchard's belt, lifting him into the air. The three of them hurried Pritchard up the stairs, while the blonde and the two brunettes followed along, circling, chattering away.

In the lobby, a beady-eyed man with a knife-blade nose and wide face, who happened to be the hotel detective, failed to notice the entrance made by Slocum and the others as they swept up the stairs past his unseeing self. He was too busy trying to look down the dress of a voluptuous beauty in a low-cut olive-green satin dress.

Once they were on the landing, Parker went on ahead, down the hall toward his room at the back of the hotel.

"Psst! Slocum!"

"What is it, Crabby? If Pritchard's coming around again,

don't hit him so hard this time. You'll soften his skull.''

''That ain't it. I just recollected where I know Parker from. I thought so before, but now that I seed him in the light, I'm sure of it!''

''So?''

''Parker is—'' Crabshaw closed his mouth, stopping just as they came within earshot of Parker. He stood outside his room, holding the door open, standing with his back leaning against it.

''This way, gents,'' he said. Slocum and Crabshaw hustled Pritchard sideways through the door and tossed him face-down across the bed. Slocum said so only Parker could hear him, ''Get rid of the girls.''

Parker shrugged, stepping into the hall and easing the door closed to keep the three women from entering. ''We're going to see to our friend for a little bit,'' he said.

''That's no party,'' one of the brunettes said accusingly.

''Not yet, but it will be. In the meantime, why don't you gals have a few drinks in the hotel bar to get you in the mood?''

''We're in the mood,'' the blonde said.

''Have a few drinks anyway.'' Parker peeled off a few greenbacks and passed them around to the ladies.

Inside, behind the closed door, Grabshaw was urgently imparting his secret to Slocum:

''Parker is—*Butch Cassidy*!''

19

Parker came in, closing the door behind him. "Nice girls," he said, grinning. "With them around, nobody's going to look at us." He locked the door.

It was a big room, two rooms really, an anteroom, with an archway opening onto the main room. The bed was in a far corner of the main room. Pritchard lay sprawled face-down across it.

Crabshaw picked up his hat from Pritchard's head and put it on his own head. Pritchard had two big lumps on the back of his skull where he'd been clipped twice. "Got himself a couple of goose eggs," Crabshaw said, chuckling.

The room was cold. The windows were open, airing it out, but there was still a thick smell of stale cigar smoke and alcohol fumes. Empty bottles were heaped on a round table in the front room. "Had a little poker game last night," Parker said.

He went to the sideboard, finding a full bottle and an empty glass. On the bed, Pritchard twitched. He worked his limbs, moaning. His eyelids twitched, as if he was blinking with his eyes shut. The lids were stretched taut across bulging eyes.

"Your friend's coming around," Parker said.

"He's got a hard head," Crabshaw said.

"Who is he?"

"Who're you?" Slocum asked. "Parker or Butch Cassidy?"

Parker smiled, then drained his glass. "Both," he said. "Parker's the name I was born with, but here out West, most folks know me as Butch Cassidy.

"I changed my name to keep from giving grief to the folks back home. Not that I'm ashamed of anything I've had to do, but you know how families are. I've been calling myself Butch Cassidy for so long, it seems like that's my real name, and George Leroy Parker is something I made up.

"The fact is, I'm not wanted for anything in Colorado, and nobody knows me here, so I thought I'd walk soft and use the Parker name to keep out of trouble.

"That is, I *thought* nobody knew me. How long have you known?"

Slocum shrugged. Crabshaw said, "I seen you up in Laramie a couple of times last year, I reckon."

Parker-Cassidy nodded. Slocum said, "I knew from the way you handled yourself at the crossing, you were no ordinary pilgrim, but I didn't know who you were until a little while ago. As far as I'm concerned, you can call yourself Parker or anything else you damned well please. It's none of my business."

"Then I'll stay Parker for now. I'm enjoying the peace and quiet that comes from being a nobody. Although I've got a feeling that might not last too much longer."

"I wouldn't be at all surprised," Slocum said.

"Where's the Sundance Kid? I thought you two was partners," Crabshaw said.

"We had to leave Cheyenne in a hurry, so we split up.

I guess he'll turn up sooner or later," Parker said. He jerked a thumb at Pritchard, asking, "Who's he?"

"Name's Pritchard," Slocum said. "He used to be a cashier in a River City bank. The bank was looted from inside and he was left holding the bag. The looters used the money to buy the Sovereign Railroad.

"The ones we gunned at the crossing were from Sovereign. They won't like us so well for putting their boys in the boneyard."

"I can stand it," Parker said mildly. "And this one?"

"Well, Pritchard knows where a lot of bodies are buried. What he knows could be useful to the Red Rock," Slocum said.

"That's who you're siding—Red Rock."

"That's right."

Crabshaw leaned forward, bright-eyed, eager. "Why don't you throw in with us, bub?"

"You're already on Sovereign's bad side," Slocum pointed out.

"I'll think about it," Parker said. "Let's bring this fellow around and hear what he's got to say."

He and Slocum took Pritchard's arms, sitting him up on the bed with his back propped up against the headboard. Pritchard groaned, his eyelids fluttering.

"Maybe some whiskey'll snap him out of it," Slocum said.

"I'll get it," Crabshaw volunteered. He lunged for the bottle that Parker had set down earlier. He filled a glass and drank it down.

"Whiskey for him, I meant," Slocum said.

"I was thirsty, dag nab it!" Crabshaw splashed some more in a glass and handed it to Slocum. Slocum poured it down Pritchard's throat, saying, "Here, drink this."

Pritchard gulped, then started coughing explosively,

choking, wheezing, his face red. "That's a waste of some fine whiskey," Crabshaw said, shaking his head sadly. He discovered that he still held the bottle, and took a long pull from it.

When Pritchard had stopped coughing, his eyes opened. Another thirty seconds, and they began to focus. He looked around wonderingly, unsure where he was. His gaze fell across Parker, then Crabshaw, with no sign of recognition. Then he saw Slocum looking down at him, sharp-eyed and sardonic.

"The man who came through the window!" Pritchard said, starting. The sudden movement brought down all the pain of a doubly conked noggin on him. He clapped his hands to his head, crying, "God! My head!"

Slocum glanced at Crabshaw, who shrugged. Slocum said, "Take it easy, Pritchard, you're among friends."

"Friends? Ha-ha!"

"I've got a grudge with the Big Three too, remember?"

Pritchard did remember. He stiffened, prying his hands away from his face, his eyes glittering, opaque. "The Big Three!"

"Claggard, Truax, and Detheroe."

"Yes! Now I remember!" His hands shot out, grabbing folds of Slocum's shirt. Crabshaw drew his gun and raised it, ready to bring it down on Pritchard's head. Slocum shook his head. Crabshaw halted, still holding the gun raised.

Slocum spoke to Pritchard in mild, reasonable tones. "You're mussing my shirtfront."

After a pause, Pritchard opened his hands and let go. "You popped one of my buttons," Slocum said.

"I . . . I'm sorry," Pritchard said.

Crabshaw said, "Just give me the word, and I'll lay him out again."

"He's all right," Slocum said. "He'd better be," he said meaningfully, giving Pritchard a hard look.

"They're coming," Pritchard said. "The Big Three. Coming here to the junction."

"They include you in on their travel plans?"

"No," Pritchard said irritatedly. "I've been tracking them. Don't forget, I know as much about them as anybody. There's plenty of people who are only too willing to talk about them, and I know who to ask.

"They're worried. The gold train contract isn't a sure thing. If Sovereign loses the race to Lonesome Canyon, the Big Three will lose everything. They'll be wiped out.

"So, they're coming in person to make sure that things work out, give it the final dirty push to tilt the scales in their favor. They're coming!"

"When?" Slocum asked.

"What—what day is this?" Pritchard asked. Slocum told him. "Soon," Pritchard said, "they're coming soon! To-morrow—no later than the next day—maybe they're already here now.

"They'll be coming down the Sovereign line on their own private train—they could be here anytime.

"We've got to be ready for them!" Pritchard swung his feet to the floor and started to rise off the bed. He looked dizzy, then sat back down.

"Take it easy," Slocum said. "When's the last time you ate?"

"I don't know, two, three days ago."

"We'll rustle up some grub for you in a minute. How'd you get here to the junction?"

Pritchard looked up out of deep eye sockets, his orbs burning, his face fanatical. "I used all the money I had—which wasn't much—to get as far west as I could. Always

I was dogging the Big Three, trying to get a line on their plans.

"I ran out of money. The last leg of the trip I made riding on top of a freight car for a couple hundred miles one night. It was the Sovereign line—funny, isn't it?

"I lay flat on top of a boxcar, clinging to the rail, afraid to move, afraid that I was going to freeze to death. Before dawn, the train stopped to take on water. I climbed down and somehow managed to get away without the railroad bulls seeing me.

"When it was light, I saw I was stuck in the middle of nowhere."

Pritchard named the site. It was about seventy-five miles away. "I walked the rest of the way," he said. "I reached town this afternoon. I knew that the Big Three would be coming here, to this hotel."

"Claggard, Truax, and Detheroe are coming here?" Slocum asked.

Pritchard nodded, then winced from the pain of moving his sore head. "They live high, wide, and handsome. Always stay at the best hotels, eat at the best restaurants. They'll come here, it's only a matter of time.

"So I decided to hide and wait for them."

"And when you find them?" Slocum asked.

Pritchard was silent. Without looking, he reached for his jacket pocket, then gave a sudden, violent start. "Where is it?!" he blurted out.

Crabshaw took Pritchard's gun out of his belt, where he'd stuck it, and dangled it tantalizingly out of reach. "Looking for this, bub?" Crabshaw asked.

"Give it to me!" Pritchard lunged for it, but Parker clapped a big hand on his shoulder and held him down, seated in place.

"That's mine! It belongs to me! You have no right—give it to me!"

"Whoa, Pritchard, whoa. You'll get it back when you behave yourself," Slocum said.

Pritchard accepted the inevitable and slumped into a dispirited posture. Beneath a fierce frown, his eyes glinted like ground glass.

"The last time I saw you, you wanted to kill yourself," Slocum said. "Now you want to kill the Big Three. What changed your mind?"

"Why should I make it easy for them?" Pritchard demanded. "Let them know what it's like to look down the wrong end of a gun before somebody else pulls the trigger.

"Maybe I'll get one of them, maybe even all three—I know that their hired men will cut me down on the spot, but I don't care, it's worth it, I'd die happy if I could know that I was taking one of them with me.

"I want them to fear."

"Don't be in such of a hurry to get yourself killed," Slocum said. "You're more dangerous alive than dead."

"What do you mean?" asked Pritchard.

"You said it yourself. You know plenty about Claggard, Truax, and Detheroe, right?"

"Yes. Oh, yes," he said softly.

"That kind of knowledge could hurt them worse than bullets," Slocum said. "You don't take down the likes of the Big Three without a plan."

"What's yours?" Pritchard asked.

"We've got to do some traveling, but first you've got to get some grub into you, so you don't faint and fall off a horse."

"Ride? Ride where?" Pritchard demanded suspiciously.

"When Sovereign wants to hang you, you go to Sovereign's enemy: the Red Rock line," Slocum said.

"That makes sense."

"Colonel Deane'll want to talk to you."

"Deane? I've heard of him . . . he's supposed to be honest. But so were the Big Three, before I learned better," Pritchard said.

Crabshaw said, "Don't fool yourself, bub. The only thing that the colonel and them three polecats have in common is that they're all trying to build a railroad to the same place."

"Is it?" Pritchard said, his upper lip curling. Then, with a sudden change of mood, he said, "Still, anybody that's against them can't be all bad."

Crabshaw rose, stretching. "Reckon I'll go see about rounding up some grub then."

"There's a kitchen in the hotel. They can put together a pretty good supper," Parker said.

Crabshaw nodded, starting for the door. "Get some whiskey too," Slocum said.

Pritchard shook his head, making a face. "No alcohol. If I have any, I'll get sick."

"Then don't drink any. That'll leave more for the rest of us."

Crabshaw went to the door, unlocking it. "Be right back," he said, opening the door and sticking his head into the corridor.

The hall was empty. Crabshaw paused, standing in the doorway, head thrust outside. His head was poised at an alert angle, listening. He frowned, concentrating.

Something was wrong—what? It wasn't a presence, but an absence. Then he got it. Noise! That was what was missing. Where was the hubbub of the crowded lobby and hotel bar, the constant babble of background noise?

Gone, all of it. Crabshaw looked back over his shoulder, into the room, where the others sat watching him.

"Funny," he said, "it sure is quiet out there. . . ."

He stuck his head into the hall again. This time when he looked, he saw three men standing at the far end of the hall, on the mezzanine overlooking the front lobby.

All three had guns in hand. One pointed it at Crabshaw and fired. He missed, because Crabshaw had already ducked his head back inside. The slug hit the door frame, sending splinters of wood and pieces of plaster flying.

The other two men opened fire an instant later, pouring lead down the hall.

Crabshaw backed up so quickly that he got tangled in his own feet and fell, sitting down hard on the floor of the anteroom. He hauled his pistol out of the holster, noticing that Slocum and Parker were already in motion.

"It sure ain't quiet no more!" he cried.

20

Now that gunfire had shattered the bubble of silence, sound rushed in to fill the vacuum. From the lobby came an eruption of shouts, screams, the chaos of mass panic, breaking glass.

Nearer was the volley of shots that came crackling down the hall, seeking the open doorway of the room. Between the blasts came pounding footsteps, closing in.

On a table in the main room, a copy of a week-old Denver newspaper lay draped over an object. Parker reached under the paper, coming up with a sawed-off shotgun.

Slocum's gun cleared the holster, as he dropped into a half-crouch, turning toward the doorway. Pritchard sat upright, clutching a headpost with one hand, dark eyes flashing in a paper-white face. Crabshaw sat on the floor, facing the open door.

The three gunmen in the hall rushed the door, shooting as they came. The angle was no good for hitting anything in the room, but the covering fire was active and noisy.

The lead gunman skittered into view, stopping short opposite the doorway. Slocum shot him twice, in the chest.

The gunman dropped to his knees in the carpeted hallway, staring wide-eyed at his shattered chest.

Crabshaw shot him and he fell back, stone dead. That slowed down the other two. They hung back, shooting into the room at an angle.

Parker crossed to the front room, sheltering against the wall to one side of the doorway. He stuck the twin barrels of the sawed-off shotgun past the door frame, into the hall at about waist-height, and cut loose.

Two booming blasts of thunder rocked the hall, spear-blades of flame lancing from the muzzle rims, followed by a cloud of smoke. The blasts were deafening, but not so much that the double-thump of two bodies hitting the floor an instant later couldn't be heard.

No gunfire—a sudden silence. Crabshaw lay flat on his belly facing the doorway, holding his gun in front of him with both hands. He wriggled, angling for a look into the hall.

Gunsmoke hung in midair in the hallway. The three gunmen's bodies lay on the floor. A flash of motion showed on the left, where the hall continued for a short distance, giving on to the back stairs.

Some men crowded at the top of the back stairs, seeing Crabshaw at the same time he saw them. Both sides fired at the same time, neither scoring.

Slugs tore up the floor at the foot of the door as Crabshaw wriggled backward, shooting with one hand, holding his hat on his head with the other.

Just before he'd ducked back inside, he'd glimpsed other figures at the opposite end of the hall. They started shooting too.

"They're coming at us from both sides!" he said. Shouted—he had to shout, to be heard over the shots.

Bullets popped, some drilling into the walls at oblique

angles. Parker reloaded, sending a blast down the hall. It didn't hit the shooters on the stairs, but it sent them dodging back, behind the cover of a blind corner. They returned fire, but not as aggressively as before. Nobody wanted to break cover and risk another blast.

Crabshaw wriggled around so he was facing the front of the building, and sent a few shots whizzing down the hall. Others shot back. A slug shattered a globe lamp set in a wall sconce in the middle of the hall. Glass blew, spewing lamp oil on the walls and ceiling. The lamp's flame blossomed, spreading over the fixture, then flaring up on the wall.

There was a lull in the shooting, in which the rustling of the flames could be heard. Parker grimaced, saying "Who?"

"Black Diamond gang!" Crabshaw said between shots. "The one outside the door, the first one shot—Timilty—I know him, he's one of the bunch."

"Who're they after?" asked Parker. "You, me—or Pritchard?"

"Maybe all three, and Crabby too," Slocum said. "I don't reckon they're too particular about who they kill."

Pritchard stood beside the bed, saying, "Give me a gun!"

In the rear wall of the main room, two high windows opened onto a balcony. A figure loomed up outside, a man-like shape glimpsed through partly curtained glass panes.

Slocum saw him, spun, and fired, drilling the glass and the man behind it. The glass shattered, falling in crystalline shards to the floor, letting in the night. The man crumpled.

Slocum flitted past the window, flattening against the wall beside it. Shots lanced through the empty window frame, fired by a second man who stood straddling the balcony rail, as if caught in the instant he was climbing over it onto the balcony.

Flame speared from his gun, underlighting his face, thick thuggish features. He missed. Slocum didn't. The other fell backward, out of sight. An instant later, he hit the street with a wet thud.

There weren't any more lurkers on the balcony. In the hall, a patch of fire four feet across burned on the wall and ceiling. It crackled, giving off an oily black smoke.

The smoke spread. From behind the closed doors of other rooms lining the halls came the sounds of clamor, commotion, and panic. A door was flung open and a woman dashed into the hall, and was cut down by a trigger-happy gunman.

"A pretty choice! Leave your room and be shot, or stay and burn!" Parker said.

Pritchard urged, "Give me a gun!"

Crabshaw fished out Pritchard's gun and gave it to him. "Man's got a right to defend himself," Crabshaw said.

"Thanks!"

"Try not to get yourself killed right off," Slocum said.

"I've stayed alive so far," Pritchard said, sullen, but stroking the gun barrel.

"To hell with that," Parker said. "Just don't get me killed."

"I know who to kill. I'm not crazy."

"Congratulations."

One of the men on the stairs leaned a little too far out from behind the corner, and Crabshaw potted him. The man fell from sight, one of his fellows cursing Crabshaw. That was followed by many bullets. At the other end of the hall, there was a sudden dramatic increase in the level of firepower.

"Fresh troops!" Crabshaw announced.

"When in doubt—retreat," Slocum said, going to the window that had been shot out. He used his gun barrel to clear the last fanged shards of broken glass clinging to the window frame.

"Maybe we can get out this way," Slocum said. "I'll see—cover me."

"Nobody's getting through this door," Crabshaw said.

Slocum stepped over the windowsill, ducking out to the balcony. Light from the room shone outside. He stepped out of it fast. The man who'd been shot through the window lay half in the light, half out of it. The upper half of his body lay in the light. His eyes were open. He looked very dead.

The room next to Parker's was dark. Slocum hugged the darkness. The balcony was built on top of the roofed-in part of the veranda. This section overlooked a side street. The building on the other side of the street was dark. The air was sweet and sharp and cold in Slocum's lungs, after the smoky indoors. Strands of smoke reached outside the room, rising.

In the side street below were some mounted men—how many Slocum couldn't tell, because the balcony partially blocked his view. But they couldn't see him either. He moved forward cautiously, edging the balcony, leaning against the railing looking down.

There was about a half-dozen riders. The horses danced, sidling, snorting, breath steaming in the chilly night air, impatient to be elsewhere.

One of the riders was a head taller than the others. That and his Texas hat marked him as Gus Andrews. Slocum could hardly believe his luck. One straight shot, and the enemy would be crippled. None of the lesser lights in the gang could take Gussie's place. Slocum raised his gun, angling for the shot. If only none of them looked up for another heartbeat—

Somebody came out the window and came up behind him—Pritchard. He saw the riders too. "Is that more of them?" he demanded, then started shooting.

Those below had seen and heard him, and they opened fire at pretty much the same time. Slocum dodged back, bullets whizzing past, horses uprearing, men cursing and shouting and shooting. Not a slug came close to Pritchard as he unloaded his gun at the surging, boiling mass below. He didn't hit anything, except maybe the ground.

Slocum collared him and hauled him back to safety, just in advance of a fusillade that tore and blistered the railing where the cashier had been standing.

He shoved Pritchard through a window into the room. It was Pritchard's luck that he happened to be standing in front of the window that had been cleared out, rather the unbroken one, since Slocum was feeling none too tenderhearted at the moment. A bullet for Gus would have solved a lot of problems. He sent Pritchard speeding on his way with a good swift kick in the tail.

Slocum climbed into the room. It was smoky, and the smoke in the hall was thicker still. Bullets drilled through the smoke, barely disturbing it.

"No good, huh?" Parker said, indicating the window.

"It's a little hot out there," Slocum said.

"It's hot in here, in case you ain't noticed," Crabshaw said. "They ain't rushing us no more, they're just gonna sit there and keep us pinned down until we burn!"

A globe oil lamp on a cabinet burned brightly, having survived all the gunplay thus far. The sight of it gave Slocum an idea. He picked it up. It was mostly full, heavy with the oil in it. He turned the wheel, causing the flame to flare up.

He told the others his plan, and set it into motion. Crabshaw held the lamp in both hands, his gun holstered. He stood on one side of the doorway. Slocum nodded.

Parker loosed a blast up the hall, toward the front of the house, then quickly dodged aside. Crabshaw pitched the oil lamp into the hall, toward the back stairs. He pitched it underhand, with both hands. It arced in midair, its angle taking it on a collision course toward the rear wall, where it would miss the gunmen sheltering on the stairs.

Slocum shot it while it was sailing through the air. It burst in a fireball, spraying burning oil down into the stairwell. There were shouts and blind shooting. Blazing oil splashed the top of the stairs and the landing, sticking like glue, spreading fast.

The stair landing swiftly filled with flame and smoke. A yellow-orange glow glimmered through the haze. It was a nice hot fire. The gunmen on the stairs could face gunfire, but not this. They retreated, coughing, stumbling, shooting to no purpose.

"Now we can't get out that way either!" Pritchard said.

"No, but we don't have to worry about our backs," Slocum said.

Bullets ripped down the hall from the front of the house, where gunmen huddled on both sides of where the hall opened onto the mezzanine. The upper half of the corridor was filled with thick smoke, the middle zone with moderately thick smoke. A good part of the hall was alight with crisply crackling tongues of flame.

"Cover me," Parker said. The man who was Butch Cassidy sent a shotgun blast scorching up the hall. It was filled with smoke and flickering flames. Slocum and Crabshaw laid down some covering fire. Anybody at the opposite end of the hall who'd stuck his head out for a peek would have had it shot off.

Parker charged into the corridor, stepping over the dead Timilty on the other side of the threshhold. He crossed to the closed door of the room opposite his and emptied the second shotgun barrel into the door lock. The blast blew out a fist-sized chunk and the door flew inward, open. Parker bulled his way into the dark, empty room beyond. The entire sequence of events had barely taken a few heartbeats.

Once inside, Parker broke the sawed-off, cleared the empties, pulled two fresh rounds from where he kept a couple of handfuls of extras in his jacket pocket, and reloaded.

The door was open and firelight shone through the doorway into the room, giving plenty of light to see by. Parker crossed to the opposite end of the room, where there were windows. He flung open a window and looked outside. There was a balcony there, a mirror image of the one outside his room. The roofed-in veranda with the balcony on top was continuous, stretching across three sides of the building. Only the fourth, rear wall was without it.

The balcony was empty. Parker went back to the doorway, signaling to the others across the hall. Bullets hummed between them, and the two fires, one in the hall and the other in the rear stairwell, arched across the ceiling, racing to meet one another.

Parker, Slocum, and Crabshaw laid down some covering fire. Slocum hurled Pritchard across the hall and into the opposite room. More shooting, and Crabshaw scurried across, bent almost double, throwing slugs down the hall. Then Slocum took a running leap and dove headfirst across the corridor, through the doorway. He hit the floor rolling and bounced to his feet, gun in hand.

There was so much smoke in the hall that visibility was limited to ten feet. That didn't stop the slugs from coming. Nobody was charging down the hall, though, not with the way the the ceiling was blazing. The flames roared.

The room across from Parker's was quickly filling with smoke. Those inside went out, through the window to the balcony, as quietly as possible.

This side of the hotel was bordered by a strip of land that had walks, lawns, and bushes. It fronted on the square, which was filled with fleeing people, wheeling horses, and a few scattered shots. Slocum went to the balcony rail. The balcony was about fifteen feet above the ground.

Some people ran out a side door, on to the veranda below. Footsteps pounded toward the front of the building. A group of men and women came into view, hurrying down a flight of side stairs, into the gardens.

That was near the front of the hotel. There was a second set of porch stairs near the rear of the building, not far below from where Slocum was standing. A man raced down those stairs, into the garden, gun in hand. Slocum hadn't known he was there until he had moved. The gunman took a few steps toward the group at the opposite end, near the square.

One of the woman saw him, gun in hand, and screamed. The others caught her by the arms and hurried her away, angling across the corner of the lot behind a screen of bushes.

The gunman checked himself, holding his fire. They weren't the ones he was looking for. He watched them go. Another voice from below called, "Lake!"

Lake was the gunman's name. He said, "It's nothing."

A third voice asked, "Is it them?"

"It ain't them," Lake said tiredly. He turned, starting for the stairs. Something caused him to look up. He saw Slocum and, nearby on the balcony, the others.

He cursed, jerking his gun up. Before he could fire, Slocum shot him. It was a tricky angle, but the round took

Lake through the top of the skull at a tangent, lofting his hat and a pancake-sized piece of his skull.

Parker was leaning over the edge of the balcony, shotgun tilted downward. Below, a doorway opened on a stairwell, the same back stairs that the gun-blasted oil lamp had set ablaze. Smoke wafted out of it. Lake and the other two were what was left of the shooters on the back stairs, who'd been forced to flee by the fire.

The shotgun bucked, two more fell, and the way was clear.

Slocum scissored one leg over the rail, then the other, then lowered himself down off the edge of the balcony, swinging down to an upright wooden beam and shimmying down it.

Parker tossed him the empty shotgun, then hung by his hands off the balcony, dropping to the soft ground not far below. Pritchard climbed down a post, nimble as a monkey, alighting easily on the lawn.

Crabshaw went to the end of the balcony, to where a drainpipe clung to the side of the building. He clung to the drainpipe and started lowering himself down. There was a groan of tearing metal as the drainpipe tore loose from the overhead gutter and swung out and down, like a giant lever being thrown by Crabshaw, who clung to the end of it. It dropped him down into a mass of bushes.

Slocum and Parker went to him. Slocum said, "You okay?"

"The bushes broke my fall. Give me a hand and help me out of here," Crabshaw said.

Slocum and Parker gripped his arms and hauled him out from amidst the mass of bushes that lay crushed beneath him. Crabshaw groaned, rubbing a sore spot. "Derned near busted my butt!"

Slocum looked around. "Where's Pritchard?"

Nowhere to be seen. "He must've slipped away when we weren't looking," Parker said.

"Slippery little cuss," Slocum said. "Well, he's on his own now. We better do like he did and vamoose."

The hotel blazed, bodies lay strewn about. "This should put us in solid with the marshal," Slocum said.

They vamoosed.

21

"It'll be light soon," Slocum said. In the east, it was already graying, leaching the darkness out of what was left of the night sky. Birds were already starting to peep and chirp in the trees, here on the top of Overlook Point, the flat-topped promontory that jutted out into the plains of Mountain Valley, south of the pass.

Up top, there was a broad flat, studded with wagon-sized boulders and thickets of woods. Slocum, Crabshaw, and Parker stood around in the rocks, trying to keep warm. Nights were cold this high up, on a ledge that was exposed to the icy winds blowing down from the mountains. The jumble of man-sized rocks provided some cover from the gusty blasts. The horses were tethered nearby, hidden in a pine thicket.

The sky was marbled with streamers and ribbons of clouds racing across it, from west to east, arcing like arrows on a celestial trajectory. Between them could be glimpsed the paling stars, fading fast as the eastern horizon brightened.

The three men paced, walking back and forth, rubbing their hands and blowing on them to keep them warm. "The great outdoors,'' Parker said. ''Give me a smoke-filled saloon any time!''

''You've got to go where the game is,'' Slocum said.

''Seems to me that the action's back in town.''

Slocum shook his head. ''Gus and company cleared out the same time that we did.''

''Anyhow, I can thank his gang for a horse.''

Crabshaw said, ''The fellow you took it from didn't have no more use for it, seeing as how he was dead.''

''He was alive until he tried to shoot me,'' Parker said blandly.

''With any luck, he'll soon be holding a reunion with the rest of the gang,'' Slocum said. The others looked at him.

''Sounds like you've got a plan,'' Parker said. ''I figured you had a reason for making us spend the night riding back and forth across the countryside, riding through the pass, and climbing a trail in the dark that a mountain goat would think twice about trying in broad daylight.''

''Thank Crabby for that. He found the trail, not me.''

''Sure,'' Crabshaw said, ''but what you wanted to come up here for in the first place is a mystery to me.''

''I'm playing a hunch,'' Slocum said, ''and now there's just about enough light for me to see if I was right.''

''What're you looking for, bub?''

''Holes, Crabby.''

''Huh?''

''Holes,'' Slocum said: A wedge-shaped rock jutted out from the tip of the formation, thrusting out into the air like the bow of a ship. It arched outward, overhanging the Red Rock Railroad line, which stretched across the flat, hundreds of feet below. The rocky fang was about fifteen feet wide at the base, and ten feet long. It was all bare rock, with nothing living there.

The false dawn came, the light in the east that precedes the sunrise. The scene was all blacks, whites, and grays. Clouds of mist rose from the valley floor, billowing upward, so that the rock fang seemed gnawing at a swirling misty void.

Slocum poked around at the base of the rock, trailed by Parker and Crabshaw. The ground bordering the rocky spur showed plenty of trampled weeds, broken branches, dried horse droppings, and other signs of life.

"Somebody's been spending some time up here," Crabshaw said, reading the signs. "More'n a couple of some-bodies, looks like."

"That's good," Slocum said, "that's what we want."

"We do? Why?" Parker asked.

"Because it tends to prove my hunch was right," Slocum said. He walked slowly along the base of the rock, studying the ground. With a sudden start, he hunkered down to examine something that had caught his attention.

Crabshaw and Parker stood over him. "That's it!" Slocum said, indicating a six-inch-wide hole in the ground. It was a regular circle, smooth-edged, clearly man-made.

Slocum moved along the base, finding another hole a few feet away from the first one. "Here's another," he said, moving further along the line, "and another!"

He rose, grinning. "So what?" Parker said, unimpressed. "They're just holes in the ground."

"Not quite—they're holes *in the rock*," Slocum said. "And putting them there was no easy job. Each one had to be drilled down deep through solid rock, and whoever did it didn't do it for fun."

"Then—why?"

"Look. The holes are drilled in a straight line, spaced a few feet apart, right where this big slab of rock juts out from the cliff. Each hole goes down nice and deep."

"I get you," Crabshaw said, nodding, eyes turned up at the corners, glittering.

"I don't," Parker said, puzzled.

"Let me explain," Slocum said. "I asked myself a question. What's the best way to stop the Red Rock line? Something that'll screw up the timetable so much that the line'll never be able to get back on schedule, causing Red Rock to lose the race.

"The bridge downriver was already wrecked once, but it's too well guarded for that to happen a second time. Even it it is wrecked, it can be rebuilt within a day.

"The same goes for derailments. If worse came to worst, you could extend the tracks around the wreck, and run a new train down the line.

"Shooting Colonel Deane, or grabbing his daughter and holding her hostage would do it, but they're both well guarded at the end of track camp.

"But there was one way to bring the line to a crashing halt. I saw it right off, and you can bet Gussie did the same. I know, because we both think the same way.

"We're standing on it. This point is tailor-made for it. All you've got to do is blast this chunk of rock off the side of the cliff, and drop a couple of hundred tons square on the tracks below. In most places, the cliffs are too far away from the line for rockfalls to do any damage, but here at the lookout, there's a juggernaut ready at hand.

"Railroads are used to blasting through hard rock. Get a crew from Sovereign up here, and a day's hard work should do it. Just drill holes in a line across the base, fill them with dynamite, and touch them off, and it'll pry the whole spur clean off the cliff."

Crabshaw and Parker both stepped to safe ground, on the far side of the line of holes. "There's no dynamite in them now—I looked," Slocum said. "You wouldn't want to leave the explosives out all night, or for a couple of nights, untended so that the caps can get wet or the wires broken by nosy varmints.

"No, you want to put them in last. Now that the holes have been drilled, all you've got to do is fill them with bundles of dynamite and give it the go.

"Now, then, Gus found out we were in town last night, so he came down from the canyon to make a try for us," Slocum continued.

Crabshaw snorted. "Found out, hell! That's why you had us hanging around town, showing ourselves—you wanted them to know we was there!"

Slocum didn't deny it. "Nothing catches fish like live bait," he said, grinning.

"No, but it can sure play hell with the bait!"

"But Gus gut hooked. He got away, but we gave him a bloody nose. He's going to be looking to got even, and what better way than by lowering the boom on Red Rock and taking it permanently out of the race?"

Parker rubbed his chin, his eyes shrewd. "You think the gang'll try today?"

"I'm counting on it," Slocum said. "The race'll be settled anyway in the next day or two, and the way things're going, Red Rock will be the winner.

"Besides, Gus is a Texan. A bloody nose won't scare him. He keeps coming at you until he gets you . . . or you get him.

"We shouldn't have long to wait. The gang's probably started up the trail by now, since they'll want to have ridden through the pass in darkness, to avoid being seen.

"Let's get ready for them."

22

The first rider topped the ledge, breaking out onto the level cliff top. He faced the sun, which was shining into his eyes. He lowered his head, tilting his hat brim so it shielded him from the direct rays. The sun was still low and shadows were long and slanting.

Behind him, the trail was narrow, forcing the rest of the gang to advance up the last of the slope in single file. Soon they were all on the ledge, in an open space ringed by boulders. On the far side of the ring was the rocky spur of Overlook Point.

Gus was there, sitting in his saddle tall and straight and fierce, like a totem pole with a hat and a gun. Silverado and Charlie Pye were there, and seven or eight others, hard-cases all. The previous night's events hadn't done anything to lighten the mood.

Among them was a balding man, pale, with clownlike tufts of ginger-colored hair. He got down off his horse and went to a packhorse that trailed his by a tow rope. The animal was laden with sacks filled with bundles of dynamite.

Some of the others got down off their horses and

stretched. Charlie Pye said, "Hurry up and get that blast set. We're gonna drop a mountain on the morning supply train."

"We'll be on time," the red-haired man said.

A shot rang out, hitting the dirt in front of the horses. The ricochet whined up and off into the rocks. A voice shouted, "Gus!"

Both shot and voice had come from somewhere in the boulders, impossible to say where. And the sun shining into the gang's faces didn't help.

But Gus knew that voice. "Slocum!" he roared. "I should've killed you a long time ago!"

"You would've if you could've!" the voice came back. "Now you're under the gun, so—be polite!"

Gus drew his gun, as did some of the others. Slocum said, "I wouldn't start shooting with all that dynamite around!"

The outlaws paused, unsure, worried. Charlie Pye was white-faced, green around the edges. "He's right, Gus! For God's sake, don't shoot!"

"Yellowbelly," Gus said, shooting him.

Up in the rocks, Crabshaw perched with his long rifle, aiming it at the sacks of dynamite. When Gus fired, so did he.

The .50 caliber impacted the explosives, and—

The cliff top blew its top. Smoke, fire, shock, chaos. Debris rained down for some time. Brisk mountain winds blew most of the smoke and grit away.

There was a smoking crater where the gang had been. Slocum, Crabshaw, and Parker emerged from behind cover and came together to inspect the damage.

"They're gonna have to call this place Bald Knob Top from now on," Crabshaw said.

"I'll get the horses, and then we'll have a date with the Big Three," Slocum said.

"What'd you say? I can't hear you, my ears are still ringing," Parker said, shaking out an ear.

Slocum crossed to the edge of the open space, coming to a wooded rise. The horses were hobbled on the other side of the rise, so its protective bulk had stood between them and the blast. He reached the edge of a stand of pines and started to duck his head to plunge in between the branches.

A click sounded, the kind made by a hammer being cocked on a gun. Slocum froze. Broken mirthless laughter sounded from above. Slocum looked up.

Caught in the net of broken tree branches, about twelve feet above the ground, was a blackened scarecrow of a gunman. He'd been caught at the edge of the blast and snatched up and flung into the trees by the shock waves. His bones were broken, his hair was burned off, his flesh was scorched, but he was alive and he held a gun pointing down at Slocum.

It was Silverado, grinning a death-mask grin. "You lose," he said.

There was a shot, drilling Silverado and dropping him out of the tree, to hit the earth with a thud.

Slocum looked behind, where Crabshaw stood, holding a smoking gun.

"Like shooting a treed possum!" Crabshaw said, chuckling.

23

"Here's where we part trails," Parker said. He, Slocum, and Crabshaw were on horseback, drifting away from the siding with the private train at the latest End of Track camp. It was midday and the railhead had extended into the pass. Across the gap, on the other side of the pass, the Sovereign line was still short of reaching the north gate.

"The colonel pays well," Parker said, riffling through a wad of large greenbacks, then stuffing it in an inside pocket.

"He said he hoped we'd always be on the same side. I think he knew who I was," Parker said, laughing. "Working for a railroad's something new for me. I'm usually on the other side. And if I hang around here for too long, the sight of those big fat railroad payrolls is likely to lead me into temptation.

"It's been fun being Parker for a while," he said, "but I can no more stop being Butch Cassidy than a tiger can change its stripes."

"Where'll you go now?" Slocum asked.

"I'm going to meet up with my partner, and then clear out of these parts pretty fast." Parker glanced back at the siding, where Clarissa Deane stood on the observation platform of the colonel's private car, watching them go.

"If I stay too long, I might start forgetting I'm Butch Cassidy," he said, his smile quirked.

Slocum nodded.

Breaking the mood, Crabshaw said brightly, "Well, we sure had us a time, Butch!"

"Sure did, old-timer. By the way," he added slyly, "Aunt Ethel was asking after you."

"After me?! What in thunder for?"

"I don't know, maybe she's sweet on you."

"Who could resist?" Slocum added dryly.

"That old crow!" Crabshaw scoffed.

"You're no spring chicken yourself, Crabby."

"No, and I don't aim to be no plucked chicken neither! But all the same, it's too bad you ain't gonna be with Slocum and me at the finish."

"Oh, you may hear from me yet," Butch Cassidy said too casually. "As a matter of fact, I was wondering if you might happen to have a stick of dynamite or two that you can spare."

"I think it could be arranged," Slocum said.

24

Late that afternoon, at the Sovereign railroad End of Track camp, the Big Three were running for their lives. They were running away from the railhead, toward their private train, which lay farther up the line, its steam engine at full pressure with an engineer in the cab waiting for the signal to go.

Behind the trio, about seventy-five yards or so behind, was an angry mob of over a hundred rough-and-ready workers, red-faced and bawling. Many held picks, clubs, spades, and other tools, shaking them menacingly at the fugitive three.

Claggard, Truax, and Detheroe. Ryan Claggard was an outdoorsman in city duds, with a smart, sharp face. He was in the best condition of the three, and ran ahead of the other two.

Josh Truax had short bristling hair and a stiff oxblood-colored mustache. Now his face was the same color as he ran huffing and puffing, his short stubby limbs working like pistons.

Detheroe trailed close at Truax's heels. He was fifty, a big man, heavyset, with a thick head of silver hair and a flowing lead-colored mustache. His mouth was a fist-sized black hole sucking air, surrounded by tight red features. He was well dressed, with long narrow feet in soft cream-colored leather boots.

They ran alongside the track, the howling mob closing in fast from behind, the rear of the waiting train ever nearer ahead. It looked as if they would reach the train ahead of the mob, if their wind held out and no one stumbled. Certainly Claggard would reach it—he was way in front.

A group of workers angled across the ground, taking a shortcut instead of following the others along the tracks. Their path brought them to the tracks at a point pretty much even with Claggard. One instant they weren't there. Then he glanced to his side again, and a half-dozen or so men were pouring down the side of the cut toward him.

His stride became unsure and he almost fell. Then his face set in stubborn lines. He hauled his gun from its holster and shot the man nearest him. He shot another. The rest broke to the sides or threw themselves flat.

The first man who'd been shot lay in the weeds, moaning. The second lay flat, motionless. The front ranks of the pursuing mob wavered, faltered, slowed, but there was still plenty of pressure from behind, pushing them forward.

Claggard stood, smoking gun leveled. "That'll show them," he said. He waved to Truax and Detheroe, who were running toward him.

"Come on, before the rabble get their nerve back," he said. He turned, starting for the train. A few paces ahead, to one side of the tracks, was an equipment shed.

A man stepped out from behind it—Austin Pritchard. He had a gun too. As soon as he saw Claggard, he opened fire, cutting him down. Claggard fell out of life with a surprised look on his face.

Pritchard stepped forward stiff-legged, his gun smoking.

Truax froze. Detheroe threw himself to the side, darting between two bushes and disappearing into a trail that wound through tangled scrub brush.

Pritchard pointed the gun at Truax. Truax squealed. Pritchard jerked the trigger, the gun clicking. It was empty.

Before Truax could faint, the first of the workers had reached him. They laid hands on him, not gently. Some of them peeled off to the side, chasing Detheroe, who was already out of sight.

Spokesman for the mob was a giant of a man with red hair and big fists. He clapped Pritchard on the back, nearly knocking him down.

"Good work, lad! You cut the dirty murdering swine down just in time!" he cried. Others crowded around Pritchard, swamping him with an excess of grim-jawed goodwill.

"We ain't been paid in weeks," the leader said, shaking his fist under Truax's nose, "and now that Red Rock's beaten us to the punch, you three dogs try to run out on us without giving us our pay!

"And you almost got away with it, if not for this fine lad here, who stepped in at the nick of time to stop your getaway! You're a hero, lad," he said to Pritchard, whom he held close to him with a big brawny arm across his shoulders, hugging him.

"That's not what happened—" Pritchard began, but the leader cut him off.

"Modest too! What'd I tell you, boys—a real hero!"

The men cheered. When they had quieted down, Pritchard tried again. "You don't understand," he said, "I've been tracking these men and—"

"Caught 'em just in time, didn't ye?! Otherwise, they'd have run out with our gold! We're powerful grateful, stranger, powerful grateful,'' the leader said, setting off another round of backslapping.

"That's a lie!'' Truax protested weakly. "Everyone of you men will be paid in full!''

"Oh, yeah?!'' the red-haired man challenged. "Then why were you and your highbinder partners running out of camp as soon as you heard Red Rock had won the race?''

"We were just hurrying to make sure that the money was safe! It's all there, every cent of the payroll, locked up safely on the train—''

Truax faltered, falling silent as he looked up the tracks.

"What train?'' the leader demanded, grabbing Truax with both hands and shaking him. "The one that's just pulling out of here?!''

The private train, the one with the fired-up locomotive at full boil, waited no longer. While the others had been absorbed in the capture of Truax, the train had lurched into motion, and was now speeding away up the line, already far beyond possible pursuit.

The whistle tooted mockingly.

Later, the train would be found standing a mile or two away, with the engineer and fireman bound hand and foot, and the safe in the Big Three's private car minus its door, which had been blown off by a stick or at the most two sticks of dynamite. The safe was empty, of course, its payroll money gone. . . .

At dusk, two mounted men met in a clearing. One was the man who called himself Butch Cassidy, the other a too-handsome blond dandy who wore his side arm gunfighter-style. The two exchanged greetings.

"Howdy, Butch.''

"Hi, Kid, long time no see.''

The other nodded. "What you got there?''

"A bagful of money, courtesy of the Sovereign Railroad. Talk about candy from a baby!"

"You haven't been sleeping," the other said admiringly. "Me neither." He reached into a saddlebag and pulled out a brick-sized packet of big bills.

"How'd you get that?" Butch Cassidy asked.

"Craziest thing," the other said. "I'm riding along the trail, no one around for miles, and suddenly some dude comes crashing out of the woods—on foot, in the middle of nowhere—pulls a gun on me, and tells me he's taking my horse!

"He must've been loco, but what could I do? He blinked, and I drew and shot him. I searched him, and found all this money on him. I guess he robbed it and was running away with it, or something."

"That must've been Detheroe," Butch Cassidy exclaimed. "Talk about bad luck! Of all the people in the world, he tries to steal a horse from the fastest gun in the West, the Sundance Kid!"

25

At sundown, Slocum and Crabshaw rode into Mountain Valley Junction, trailing on a string a third horse, across the back of which was draped a blanket-wrapped body. On their way into town, they met the marshal.

"I hope I'm not going to have any trouble with you," Slocum said.

"The Red Rock line's in the saddle now, so we're all pals," the marshal said, grinning broadly. "Anyhow, I'm busy running out that Sovereign herd. Those boys are out of a job, and out of the money, so they'll have to move on.

"But you boys are always welcome. We're on the same side now."

"Phooey," Crabshaw said while the lawman was still in earshot. He and Slocum rode on, halting in front of the cafe. Somebody went inside and got Eileen Barrett, who stood on the plank sidewalk, hands on hips.

Slocum pulled back the blanket so the head was showing, then grabbed a fistful of hair and jerked it up, so the face was in the light.

"Silverado," he said. She nodded slowly. He let go of the hair, the head slumping down into the shadows.

"So, it was you after all, cowboy," she said.

"Well, no. You see, the joke's on both of us," Slocum said. "It was Crabby here who got Silverado."

She turned to look at Crabshaw, but otherwise didn't bat an eye. "So you're the one," she said. "This is your big night, Grandpa. I always pay my debts.

"You go get yourself cleaned up and take a shave and a bath and come back here, and I'm going to give you all my sweet, sweet loving, you straight-shooting little old man."

"A bath!" Crabshaw squawked, horrified. "To hell with that! I ain't changing myself nohow for nobody, not even you, ma'am!

"Besides, I heard that too much soap and water can weaken you!"

Crabshaw shuddered. Eileen Barrett shrugged. "I'll go take the body down to the jailhouse," Crabshaw said. "They can figure out what to do with it. Then I'm gonna get me a drink, no, a whole mess of drinks!"

"Go ahead, I'll catch up with you," Slocum said.

"Sure, when you're done making sheep-eyes at that red-headed woman," Crabshaw said. He rode off, trailing the horse-and-body, muttering to himself:

"A bath! Crazy ideas these women get!"

A few hours later, though, a very much changed Crabshaw came striding up to the cafe. He'd had a few drinks, thinking about the woman, her fire hair and full red lips and figure of passion. . . . He'd had a few more drinks, but hadn't been able to stop thinking about her. Somehow, he'd managed to stumble into a place specializing in hot baths, and was now freshly scrubbed, pink skin gleaming, white hair and billy-goat beard neatly trimmed, and was even wearing clean new clothes.

"That redheaded gal's worth it!" he'd said en route to

claim his prize. Now he stopped short in front of the cafe—
it was dark, the door locked, a CLOSED sign hanging in the
window.

Thinking that he'd seen someone inside, Crabshaw went
around to the side of the cafe, standing on tiptoes to peer
in through a partly open window.

He heard hard breathing, panting, sighs, and groans. In
the dimness of the cafe, he saw Slocum and the woman,
their bodies nude, glowing, writhing. She lay on her back
on a counter, while he stood facing her, her legs wrapped
around his waist as his hips thrust, driving into her, while
she lifted her ass up off the counter to meet him more than
halfway with each breathless stroke.

Somebody tapped Crabshaw on the shoulder, surprising
him so that he almost jumped out of his skin. It was Aunt
Ethel, dressed up in her go-to-town clothes.

"I thought it was you ducking into this alley, Mr. Crabshaw," she began. "I've been wanting to talk to you
and—"

Love cries from inside came through the window. "Why,
you naughty man," Aunt Ethel said roguishly, archly lifting
an eyebrow while giving Crabshaw a come-hither stare that
made his blood run cold.

"What you need is a woman more your own age, my
dear Mr. Crabshaw. Won't I do?"

"Thunderation!"

JAKE LOGAN

TODAY'S HOTTEST ACTION WESTERN!